Jessi and the Jewel Thieves

**Other books by
Ann M. Martin**

Ma and Pa Dracula
Yours Turly, Shirley
Ten Kids, No Pets
Slam Book
Just a Summer Romance
Missing Since Monday
With You and Without You
Me and Katie (the Pest)
Stage Fright
Inside Out
Bummer Summer

BABY-SITTERS LITTLE SISTER series
THE BABY-SITTERS CLUB mysteries
THE BABY-SITTERS CLUB series
(see back of the book for a more complete listing)

Jessi and the Jewel Thieves
Ann M. Martin

AN
APPLE
PAPERBACK

SCHOLASTIC INC.
New York Toronto London Auckland Sydney

Cover art by Dan Brown

ISBN 0-590-44959-1

12 11 10 9 8 7 6 5 4 3 2 1   3 4 5 6 7 8/9

Printed in the U.S.A.   28

First Scholastic printing, April 1993

The author gratefully acknowledges
Ellen Miles
for her help in
preparing this manuscript.

"New York, New York," I sang, really belting out the words. "These little-town blues, are melting away," I went on as I opened my closet. I glanced inside, trying to decide which of my clothes might possibly pass for cool in the big city. After a minute, I shrugged. My clothes don't even pass for cool in my little town. There was no way any New Yorkers were going to mistake me for a fashion model.

I couldn't believe I was actually going to spend another weekend in the Big Apple. Me, Jessi Ramsey, an eleven-year-old in the sixth grade at Stoneybrook Middle School. I was going to be on my own in the most exciting city in the world!

Well, not on my own, exactly. I'd be staying with my friend Stacey McGill, who was going to be visiting her father in his Manhattan apartment. Stacey's parents are divorced, and she lives with her mother here in Stoneybrook,

Connecticut, which is the little town I was just referring to. But Stacey's dad still lives in New York, where Stacey grew up. She visits him fairly often, and this time I was going along.

But I wasn't going to be spending all my time with Stacey. The reason I was going was so that I could attend a ballet at Juilliard. What's Juilliard? Only one of the best music and dance schools in the world, that's all. And why was I going to a performance there? Well, because this boy I know named Quint Walter was going to be dancing in it, and he'd invited me to come and see him perform.

Ballet is my passion in life. I go to a special ballet school in Stamford, which is a city near Stoneybrook. I have been studying ballet for years now, and while I may not be at the Juilliard level, I'd have to say that I'm pretty good. I mean, I don't want to sound self-centered, but I have worked really hard at my dancing, and the work has paid off. I have actually danced the lead role in several big performances.

Still, ballet isn't the only thing in my life. I like to do a lot of things, for example: I like to be with my family, which consists of my baby brother Squirt, my eight-year-old sister Becca, my parents, and Aunt Cecelia. Oh, and a hamster named Misty. I also love to read, especially horse stories, and I like to spend time with my best friend Mallory Pike, who also loves horse stories. Another of my favorite activities is baby-sitting. I sit for my brother and sister, of course, but I also sit for a lot of kids who live nearby. In fact, I belong to a group called the Baby-sitters Club, and the other members of that club are my good friends. Stacey is a member, and so is Mallory.

I have been to New York before, along with the other members of the BSC (that's what we call our club). In fact, I met Quint during one of those trips. I had gone to Lincoln Center to see the New York City Ballet dance *Swan Lake*, and the performance was totally amazing. And then, to top it off, I found myself sitting next to this incredibly cute boy. He turned out to be a dancer, too, and we hit it off right away. In fact, Quint was the first boy I ever kissed! (Not that I kissed him that day. I got to know him a little better, first.)

I was feeling kind of nervous about seeing Quint this time around. We have had what you might call a long-distance romance, and it has been fun, but lately I've been wondering if it might be better for us to just be friends. It isn't easy having a relationship with someone you see only once in a while. For example, I'm never sure how "true" to Quint I'm supposed to be. I have gone to two dances with this seventh-grade boy named Curtis Shaller, who I really like. Does that make me a two-timer? Does Quint also go out with other girls down there in New York? These things have never been clear to me.

"I'm going to have to talk to him about this," I said to myself as I poked through my sweater drawer. "After all, I'm only eleven, and maybe I shouldn't really *have* a steady boyfriend, much less one who lives so far — "

"Who are you talking to?"

I stopped in mid-sentence and whirled around to see Becca standing in the doorway, giggling at me.

"I'm talking to me, myself, and I," I said, smiling. "That's *whom.*"

"I thought only crazy people did that," she said.

"Well, I guess I'm crazy, then," I said. "What are you up to?"

"I heard you singing before," she said. "That song about Yew Nork."

"I laughed. You mean New York," I said. "New York, New York!" I sang out. "That one?"

"Right," she said. "Will you teach it to me?"

"Sure. Come on, I'll show you the dance that goes with it, too." I grabbed her and we faced the mirror. We sang and high-kicked our way through three verses, looking like chorus girls in a Broadway show.

Afterward, we flopped on the bed. "Whew," I said. "That was fun."

"Yeah," said Becca. But she didn't sound too happy.

I glanced over at her. She was chewing on her thumbnail and looking as if she were about to cry. Kids can change their moods so fast!

"What's the matter?" I asked her.

"Nothing," she said, but she was still frowning.

"Come on, Becca, you can tell me," I said. "What's wrong?"

She sighed. "I'm being abandoned by my own family, that's what's wrong," she replied. A tear began to glisten in the corner of her eye. "You're going to New York this weekend, and Mom and Dad and Squirt and Aunt Cecelia are all going to that wedding. And I'm going to be left behind, all by myself!" Her lip quivered, and the tear fell. "Nobody loves me," she said, giving a little sniff.

"Oh, Becca, of course we love you," I said, reaching over to give her a hug. "And nobody's abandoning you, or leaving you alone. You're going to be staying with the Pikes." I smiled at her. "You'll have fun there."

"Will not," she said, sniffing again.

I could understand why Becca was feeling a little left out. It was true that everyone else in the family was going away that weekend. See, my parents and Aunt Cecelia had been invited to this big family wedding in Massachusetts. But it was the kind of wedding that kids aren't invited to. (Squirt, our baby brother, wasn't invited either, but he was too young for my parents to leave behind. He would spend the day of the wedding at the hotel with a baby-sitter.)

For me, the wedding came at the perfect time. I had been nervous about asking my parents if I could go to New York, and I had been *shocked* when they agreed immediately. But the fact was that they were probably just relieved to know that I had somewhere to go that weekend, so that they wouldn't have to figure out what to do with me. Anyway, once I had a place to go, the rest was easy. Mallory's parents had invited Becca to stay at their house. I guess it doesn't make much difference to them if another kid is in the house, since Mallory has *seven* brothers and sisters!

"But why do I have to stay with the Pikes?" asked Becca, sounding a little whiny. "If I have to be abandoned, I want to stay with Charlotte." Charlotte Johanssen is Becca's best friend.

"Becca," I said, trying to be patient. "Charlotte and her parents are going away this weekend, too. You know that."

"Everybody's going away," she wailed. "Everybody but me. Even Squirt gets to go! It's not fair." She buried her face in my pillow.

"Squirt is only going because he's too little to be away from Mom and Dad," I said, rubbing her back. "And he's *not* going to the wedding. He's going to stay with a sitter, at the hotel."

Squirt's real name, in case you're wondering, is John Philip Ramsey, Jr. A big name for a baby, right? That's what the nurses thought when he was born. He was the smallest baby in the hospital's nursery, so they nicknamed him Squirt, and the name has stuck. Now he's not such a squirt anymore. He's learning to walk and talk and feed himself, and he's incredibly cute.

Squirt was born in Oakley, New Jersey, which was where Becca and I were also born. We lived there until the beginning of this school year, when my father's company transferred him to a branch office in Stamford. Sometimes I miss Oakley — or at least I miss certain things about it. For one thing, back in Oakley we lived on the same street as my grandparents, two of my uncles, three aunts, and tons of cousins. One of my cousins,

Keisha, was my best friend. She lived right across the street. I never felt lonely. I also never felt different, which is something I feel quite often here in Stoneybrook. Why? Because my family is African-American. Back in Oakley, there were plenty of other black families. But there aren't too many here. In fact, when we first moved to Stoneybrook, certain individuals weren't too happy about our living here. Some people say that racism comes from ignorance, or from fear, and I think that's true. Several Stoneybrook residents had never really *met* a black person before! Now that people have gotten to know us, they're generally a lot nicer. Still, I do feel different sometimes.

"*Jessi!*" Becca was trying to get my attention.

"What is it?" I asked.

"I think I know a secret," she said. Becca is crazy about secrets.

"Oh?" I asked. "Are you going to tell me what it is?"

She nodded. "Mom and Dad are only *pretending* I'm not coming to the wedding," she said. "At the last minute, they're going to take me with them."

"Uh, Becca — " I was about to tell her that her "secret" sounded more like a wish, but then I saw how hopeful she looked and I couldn't stand to say it. "Maybe," I replied

8

carefully. "But I don't think so. They'd *like* to take you, but I don't think they can." Her face fell. I felt awful. "But you're going to have a terrific time at the Pikes'," I said. "You always have fun over there, remember?" I hoped I didn't sound as desperate as I felt. Becca looked crestfallen. "Come on and smile for me," I said. I reached out and hugged her again.

"Jessi!" I heard my aunt call from downstairs. "It's already quarter to five, and you promised to go to the store for me before your club meeting. You better get a move on!"

I jumped up. I'd almost forgotten that it was Wednesday, and I had to be at my BSC meeting by five-thirty. "Okay, Aunt Cecelia," I called back. "Be right down!" When Aunt Cecelia speaks, I listen. She doesn't like for people to ignore her orders — I mean, her requests. In fact, Becca and I used to have a mean name for her: Aunt Dictator. Actually, she's not so bad anymore. But when she first came to live with us this year (when my mother went back to work and needed help with Squirt), it took her awhile to understand how responsible and mature I can be. She treated me like a baby! And she wasn't too nice to Becca, either.

"Yes, sir — ma'am — Aunt Dictator!" I

said, under my breath. I grinned at Becca, hoping she would smile back.

And she did. At least, she gave me something *resembling* a smile. "That's better," I said. I gave her a squeeze and ran downstairs, humming "New York, New York" as I went.

CHAPTER 2

Stacey and I arrived at the BSC meeting at exactly the same moment. We walked into Claudia Kishi's room — the official headquarters of the BSC — and saw that everyone else was already there.

"Hey," said Claudia. "It's the jet-setters. Off to fabulous New York for the weekend. Right, dahlings?"

"But of course," replied Stacey, grinning and striking a pose. "And then next week we're off to Paris for the start of the fashion season." She looked over at me. "Fabulous, isn't it?"

"Divine," I said. We cracked up. It was funny, but I did feel like a real sophisticate, knowing that I would soon be walking down Fifth Avenue. "I can't wait," I told Stacey. "By this time on Friday we'll be on our way!" We were going to miss a BSC meeting that day — something I hate to do — but the train we were taking left at four-thirty, so there was no way around it.

Just then, Kristy checked the digital clock, which had just flipped to five-thirty, tapped her pencil on the arm of her chair, and called, "Order! And that means everybody, jet-setters *and* us hicks!" It was time for the meeting to start.

Here's how the club works: we meet in Claudia's room every Monday, Wednesday, and Friday, from five-thirty until six. During those times, parents can call us to set up jobs, and believe me, they do call. We always have plenty of business. At first the club advertised with fliers and the occasional ad in the paper, but now that's hardly ever necessary. We have lots of regular clients, and we're always getting new ones who have heard about us from our satisfied customers.

The idea for the club was Kristy's, which is why she's the president. Actually, she's also the president because she's just naturally a good leader. She knows how to organize people and how to inspire them, and she's always coming up with awesome ideas for projects. Kristy can be a little bossy at times, but I guess that goes along with the other parts of her personality.

Kristy is short for her age (she's thirteen and in the eighth grade, like everyone else in the club except for Mal and me), and she has brown hair and eyes. She does *not* take advantage of the fact that she is thirteen, however. If I were thirteen, I'd be wearing all kinds of cool outfits and fixing my hair a different way every day. But not Kristy. She wears practically the same outfit all the time: jeans, turtleneck shirt or T-shirt (depending on the weather), and running shoes. And she never does anything interesting with her hair. I bet she hardly bothers to look in the mirror in the morning. Which is not to say that she's not pretty: she is. She just doesn't put any work into it.

Anyway, enough about Kristy's looks. Let me tell you about her family. It's an interesting one. First of all, Kristy's dad took off when Kristy was very young, leaving Mrs. Thomas to raise Kristy and her three brothers (two older, one younger) on her own. Those times weren't easy. But eventually Mrs. Thomas met and married this great guy, Watson Brewer. He's a millionaire, and I'm not joking. The Thomases moved across town and into Watson's mansion. It's lucky that Watson owned a mansion since a lot of people are now living in that place. See, besides Kristy and her three brothers (David Michael, Charlie, and Sam), there are Watson's two children from his first marriage, Andrew and Karen. They don't live at the mansion full time, but they're there a lot. Then there's Emily Michelle, who's two and a half years old and cuter than anything. She's Vietnamese. Kristy's mom and Watson adopted her soon after they got married. And after Emily Michelle arrived, Nannie (Kristy's grandmother) came to live at the mansion, too, just to help out.

As you can imagine, it's a pretty busy household. And I haven't even told you about their pets yet! (They have an old cat, a puppy, and two goldfish.)

So Kristy's pretty busy, with that big family and being president of the BSC. Plus she coaches a softball team called the Krushers. But Kristy's not Supergirl. She has her limits. Not long ago, she ran for president of the eighth grade, but she found that she had to quit partway through her campaign because she was just overloaded with activities. Still, Kristy is the best idea-person in the BSC. Here are a few of her other ideas: First, the club notebook. That's where we keep a record of every sitting job we go on. (We each write up our own jobs.) Then we read it every week, to keep informed about our clients and any special problems that the kids we sit for might be having. Second, the club record book. That's where we keep all the club information and scheduling information, so we can tell at a glance who's free for a particular job. And finally, our Kid-Kits, which are boxes (we've decorated them so they look way cool) filled with toys and games that we — or our brothers and sisters — have outgrown. We also add new stickers and markers and things. So even though all the toys aren't new, they're new to the kids we sit for, and they're always a big hit.

Sometimes I wonder what the BSC would be like without Kristy. I don't think it could exist!

But she's not the only important member of the club.

Claudia is the vice-president. We meet in her room because she's the only member of the club with her own phone *and* a private line. That's important, because otherwise we'd be tying up somebody else's line with our calls. Claudia's other duties include (officially) answering calls during non-meeting times and (unofficially) providing junk food for our meetings.

Claud considers it a pleasant part of her job to have junk food on hand. Why? Because she loves the stuff. Nothing makes her happier than cruising the aisles of a candy store or convenience mart, deciding between Munchos and Doritos, Kit-Kats and Snickers, Life Savers and Jawbreakers.

Claudia does not look like a person who

practically lives on junk food. She has a flawless complexion, and she's not at all overweight. In fact, she's gorgeous. She's Japanese-American, with long black hair and almond-shaped eyes. And she is one of the best dressers at Stoneybrook Middle School. She has a real flair for putting together trendy, one-of-a-kind outfits, and for fixing her hair in amazing styles.

Claud is an incredibly talented artist. She paints, she draws, she sculpts, she makes jewelry. You name it, she does it, and she does it well. She just loves art. What she doesn't love is school, and unfortunately that shows in her grades. She's one of those people who is always having to hear her parents say things like, "If you would just apply yourself," and "You have so much potential." She also has to hear teachers say, "Are you really Janine's sister?" Claudia's sister Janine is a real live genius. You know that lady who answers brain-teasers in the newspaper? The one who's supposed to be the smartest woman in the world? Well, Janine will probably replace her when she decides to retire. Luckily for Claudia, Mr. and Mrs. Kishi are good parents, and I think they try not to compare their daughters when it comes to grades.

The secretary of the BSC is Mary Anne Spier, who is Kristy's best friend. You might think she would be as loud and outgoing as Kristy is, but she's not. She's extremely shy and sensitive. They do look alike, though: Mary Anne has brown hair (although she recently got it cut), and brown eyes and is also short for her age.

As secretary, Mary Anne takes care of that record book I told you about. Her neat, even handwriting fills every page, and she does a perfect job of keeping track of all our appointments. I think she has the hardest job in the BSC, but she seems to like it.

Mary Anne's mom died a long, long time ago, and Mr. Spier was the one who brought up Mary Anne (their only child). I guess he was worried about being a single parent, so he kind of overdid it. He was very, very strict about what Mary Anne could wear, and how she could fix her hair and that kind of stuff. But he's loosened up now, and Mary Anne has become a trendier dresser. (She'll never compete with Claudia, though!)

Mary Anne has a kitten named Tigger, and a cute boyfriend named Logan Bruno. And not too long ago she also acquired a stepsister! Not just a stepsister, but a best friend and a co-member of the BSC named Dawn Schafer. Here's how it happened: Dawn grew up in California, but her mother had grown up in Stoneybrook. And when Dawn's parents got a divorce, her mom decided to move back to Stoneybrook, bringing Dawn and Dawn's younger brother, Jeff, with her.

Dawn and Mary Anne became friends soon after Dawn moved here, and soon after that they discovered that their parents had been high school sweethearts! Mary Anne's dad and Dawn's mom started to date again, and before long they were married. Isn't that a romantic story?

Dawn, by the way, is the BSC's alternate officer. That means she can fill in whenever any other officer can't make it to a meeting. For example, on Friday she'd take over Stacey's job.

Dawn has long, long pale blonde hair (it's almost white, really) and big blue eyes. She dresses in this way cool casual style, and she is very mellow and laid back. She's also a health-food nut, and will not touch any of the snacks that Claudia provides. Instead, she usually brings an apple or some stone-ground wheat crackers to our meetings.

When Dawn moved here, she moved into this neat old farmhouse with a secret passage and maybe even a ghost. Now Mary Anne and her dad live there too. But unfortunately, Dawn's brother does not live there. Jeff just couldn't adjust to life in Stoneybrook, and he ended up going back to California to live with his dad. Dawn misses him like crazy, but she understands. She wasn't nuts about Connecticut, either, when she first arrived. She hated the snowy cold weather for one thing. But I think being part of the BSC has made all the difference, and now Dawn considers Stoneybrook her home (or one of her homes).

I haven't told you yet about the treasurer of the BSC. That's Stacey, the one I was going to New York with. She's a math whiz, so her job is a breeze for her. She keeps track of the money in our treasury, and also collects our dues. We pay dues every Monday, and even though it's just a small amount we always give Stacey a hard time. We hate to part with our money, and she loves to collect it and save it up! She likes the idea of having a little "nest egg" set aside for a rainy day, but we always end up spending what we save. For one thing, we pay Kristy's older brother to drive her to meetings, since she now lives too far away to walk to Claud's. We also use it to buy stuff like Magic Markers and stickers for our Kid-Kits. And once in a while, we have a pizza bash — that is, if we can worm the money out of Stacey!

Stacey is Claudia's best friend, and they definitely share a certain sophistication that the rest of us lack. Since Stacey grew up in New York City, she's very cosmopolitan. She's always doing the latest thing to her blonde hair, whether it's a perm or a body wave or rolling it up on little rubber things. She wears makeup and nail polish (often with sparkles in it) and she dresses like she just stepped out of a magazine.

There's one thing about Stacey that you'd never guess by looking at her: She's a diabetic. In case you don't know anyone with diabetes, let me explain. It's a disease in which your body doesn't produce this stuff called insulin, which helps digest sugars. So, to deal with her diabetes, Stacey has to A: watch her diet very, very carefully and hardly ever eat sweets, and B: give herself shots of insulin every day. Stacey doesn't seem to mind any of this too much. I guess she's used to it. I have to say that A would be nearly impossible for me, even though, as a ballet dancer, I *should* eat that way, and as for B — well, I can't even imagine B.

I bet you're wondering what my BSC job is. Well, both Mallory and I are junior officers, which simply means we take on many of the afternoon sitting jobs, since neither of us is allowed to sit alone at night (except for our families). Anyway, this frees up the older BSC members for night jobs.

I've told you a little about Mallory, but let me fill you in on the rest. She has red hair and freckles, braces and glasses. I happen to think she's very cute, but she won't listen to me. She'd like to wear contacts, get her braces off, and become glamorous. And I bet she will, someday. It's tough being eleven and having to be patient about these things. We both have a lot of trouble with it.

Mal's great with kids, which is lucky considering the size of her family. And, like me, she has ambitions. She'd like to be a writer and illustrator of children's books. Since she's talented and determined, her dream will probably come true.

There are two other members of the BSC, our associate members. They don't come to meetings, but they're on standby to fill in or help out. One of them is Logan Bruno, Mary Anne's boyfriend. The other is Shannon Kilbourne, a girl from Kristy's new neighborhood.

Whew! Now you know all about the BSC and its members. But what you *don't* know is how busy that Wednesday's meeting was. We hardly had time to eat the Ruffles Claudia was passing out, much less try out Stacey's new Melon Mist nail polish. Everybody had babysitting news to discuss, and the phone rang every two minutes.

"Mal and I are going to be pretty busy on Saturday while you guys are living it up in

New York," said Mary Anne, looking at Stacey and me. "We're sitting at the Pikes' — for *eight* kids, since Becca will be there, too."

"And I'm going to be sitting at the Pikes' on Sunday," said Claud. "But not for eight kids, luckily."

"Right," said Mal. "Only four. Mom and Dad are taking us older kids to a concert in Stamford that night. We've had the tickets for over a month. I can't wait! We're going to hear this jazz band, and my dad actually went to college with the drummer, so we'll get to go backstage and everything."

"Cool!" I said, even though it didn't sound nearly as cool as what *I* would be doing that weekend. "Well, I hope you all have good luck with Becca this weekend," I went on. "She's not doing too well lately." I filled them in on why Becca was upset, but nobody seemed too worried. They were sure she'd get over it, and by the time our meeting ended they had just about convinced me, too. As I headed home after our meeting, my mind was less on Becca and more on my big weekend in New York. I couldn't wait!

CHAPTER 3

Friday afternoon arrived at last. I was finally packed, which hadn't been easy. For three days I'd been putting clothes into my suitcase and then pulling them back out, since I was so unsure about what to bring. I must have called Quint five times to ask his advice on what I would need, and I called Stacey about every hour on the hour.

Mom had loaned me her best necklace, which was made of these shiny black beads called jet. And Mal had loaned me a way cool black sweater with geometric designs in primary colors. I'd been tempted to ask Claud if I could borrow her leopard-print jean-jacket, but I knew that was a bit much. I wasn't sure I could carry it off, anyway. I just don't have the style, or the attitude, or whatever it is Claudia has that lets her wear things like that without looking silly.

Anyway, I was all set. I had an outfit to

wear when I was just walking around (my best jeans, little black boots, and Mal's sweater), clothes to wear while I was lounging at Stacey's father's apartment (pajamas, robe, slippers), and something fancy to wear to Quint's dance concert (a black velvet dress I'd received on my birthday). Plus, I'd packed three books, my clock radio, shampoo and conditioner, a raincoat, and my ballet gear — just in case I had time for some stretching and practicing.

My dad grunted as he lifted my bag into the trunk of the car. "What've you got in here?" he asked. "A set of encyclopedias?"

"Dad," I said, laughing in spite of myself. "I just want to be sure I have everything I might need."

"I think your mother had the same idea when she packed for Squirt," he said. "We could stay in Massachusetts until he's ready for kindergarten!" He showed me Squirt's diaper bag, which was overflowing with diapers, bibs, toys, graham crackers, and pacifiers. I laughed again.

My dad ran back inside to get his own suitcase, and passed Becca on the way. She was lugging her Little Mermaid duffel bag, which seemed to be stuffed as full as it could get. I guess nobody in my family has heard of traveling light.

"Can you help me fasten this?" she asked. "It won't stay shut."

I took it from her and worked on the zipper. There was no way it was going to close. "You're going to have to take some things out," I said, opening it up wide to see what she might be able to do without. "Hey, Becca," I said, when I spied her red satin party dress. "What's this for?" I didn't think she was going to be needing *that* at the Pikes'.

"It's for the wedding," answered Becca, in a small, hopeful voice.

Uh-oh. This was not a good sign. Apparently Becca still hadn't given up hope. I was about to give her a gentle, sisterly talk about how we can't always do what we *want* to do, but I didn't get the chance.

"Everybody ready?" asked my father from behind me. My mom and Aunt Cecelia tossed their overnight bags into the trunk. Mom stuck Squirt into his car seat, and then the rest of us piled into the car. The plan was for us to drive together to the Pikes', where Becca and I would get out. I would make sure someone was there to greet her, and then walk through the Pikes' backyard to Stacey's house. My parents and Squirt and Aunt Cecelia would drive on toward Massachusetts.

"Here we are!" said my father, pulling up

in front of the Pike house a few minutes later. "Now, I want you girls to have a fun weekend. Jessi, you be careful down there in the big city. And Becca, be sure to mind your manners while you're staying with the Pikes."

Becca burst into tears. "I don't *wanna* stay here!" she bawled.

"Hmmph!" said Aunt Cecelia. She doesn't have a lot of patience with this kind of thing.

Mom exchanged looks with me, gave me a quick hug and a kiss, and then got out to help Becca out of the car. I heard her murmuring comforting words as I pulled our bags out of the trunk.

"Hey, Becca," called Mallory from the front porch. "I'm so glad you're here. We're just about to have a scavenger hunt! Whose team do you want to be on?"

Becca ignored her. She just sobbed harder. My mother looked a little desperate. "We have to get going," she said to me. Then she turned to Becca. "You're going to be just fine. Look, Mallory is waiting for you."

"I don't care!" cried Becca, her voice muffled by Mom's coat. "I'm not staying."

Mom gently pried Becca's arms from around her neck. "I'm sorry, honey, but we have to go now. You be a good girl." She stood up and I took her place with Becca. " 'Bye!" she said, backing away. "I'll bring you a present,

I promise," she added, wanting Becca to smile. Finally, Mom gave up and climbed into the car.

Mallory trotted down the driveway and stood with Becca and me. Becca was still sobbing. "Becca," I said, "I have to go, too. You'll have a lot of fun with Mallory." I hugged her tight and then stood up. "She's all yours," I said to Mallory, with a little smile. "Good luck!"

"Have a great trip," said Mal. "Write me a postcard."

"I'll be back before you get it," I said.

"I know. But write one anyway." She bent to hug Becca.

"See you," I said. " 'Bye, Becca." I headed through the backyard to Stacey's, trying not to hear Becca's sobs. I looked back once and caught a glimpse of her tear-stained face, and then I didn't look again. Poor Becca. She was going to be fine. I knew that. But there was no way to tell her so. She'd just have to find out on her own.

I lugged my overnight bag onto Stacey's porch. My raincoat was slung over my shoulder and another, smaller bag was under one arm. I rang the bell.

"Jessi!" said Stacey, when she answered the door. "How long are you planning to stay in New York, anyway?"

"Uh, just the weekend," I replied.

"It looks like you're going for a month, with all that stuff," she said. "I don't think you really want to carry so much junk around while you're there. Let's see what we can leave behind."

We sorted through my things and I ended up leaving the raincoat (rain wasn't forecast, and Stacey said she could lend me a jacket if a sudden storm came up), two of the books (Stacey pointed out that I wouldn't have much time to read), the clock radio and the shampoo and conditioner. I hefted the overnight bag again. "You're right," I said. "That's a lot better."

Just then Claudia, Dawn, and Mary Anne rode up Stacey's driveway on their bikes. "We're coming to the station with you," said Claud. "We wanted to see you off before our meeting starts."

"It's going to be so weird to have a meeting without you guys," said Mary Anne.

"You'll survive it, I'm sure," Stacey wise-cracked. "Just don't spend all the money in the treasury as soon as my back is turned."

"As interim treasurer," said Dawn, "I'll make sure they don't clean out the bank." She saluted.

"Okay, girls," called Stacey's mom from the

porch. "Let's get going. You've got a train to catch!"

We drove to the station and ended up standing around for about fifteen minutes, since the train was late. We were clustered underneath the sign that said NEW YORK BOUND TRAINS. What is it about waiting for a train when people are seeing you off? Nobody ever has a *thing* to say to anyone else, and you feel so awkward. Everybody keeps glancing down the track, looking for the train.

And that's what we were doing. Once in a while someone would say something like, "Be sure to eat one of those big hot pretzels you can buy from the carts on the street," or "Say 'hi' to Bloomingdale's for me!", but in between, was this nervous silence. I was relieved when an announcement blared over the loudspeaker. "The 5:05 train bound for New York will be leaving on track 2. Two minutes to boarding time."

We all hugged each other. Stacey and I picked up our bags and waited for the train to pull in. Then we climbed aboard. We were finally on our way.

The train picked up speed and started to clack along the tracks. I watched out the window as we passed by the Stoneybrook landmarks, but within minutes the landscape was unfamiliar and actually kind of boring. I started to think about the things I'd be doing that weekend: dinner with Quint's family, the ballet on Saturday night, and lots of walking around and seeing the sights and eating delicious food and shopping. I suddenly remembered a really cool store that Stacey had taken us to last time we were in New York, but I couldn't remember the name. I wanted to go there again, though, so I turned to Stacey, who had been sitting quietly, probably thinking about her own weekend plans. "Hey Stace," I said. "When we get to New York — "

"Hey, Jessi," she said, at exactly the same time. "When we get to New York — "

We both stopped short and cracked up. I touched her arm quickly and said, "Owe me a Coke." That's what we do now when two people say something at the same time: the first one to touch the other and say that wins the Coke. (In Stacey's case, a diet Coke.)

"What were you going to say?" I asked.

"Just that when we get there, I want you to stick close by me and watch what I do. You're not used to the city, and it can be pretty overwhelming."

I could tell that Stacey was feeling responsible for me. Not because I was younger, but just because I wasn't familiar with the city. It was sweet of her to worry. "I will," I said.

"What were *you* going to say?" she asked.

"I was trying to remember the name of that awesome store we went to last time," I said. "You know, the one where Claudia bought that mirror that screams when you look into it?"

"Mythology," said Stacey. "But guess what. Bad news. It closed awhile ago. We should go to Think Big, though. You'd like that store. It has gigantic versions of everything. It is *way* cool."

"Great," I replied. Then we sank into silence. I started to think about the weekend again, and about seeing Quint. I'd been trying to figure out what I wanted to say to him about our "relationship," and when I should talk to him. I'll admit I was pretty nervous, but there on the train I made a resolution: I'd have The Talk with him that night when I was at his family's house for dinner. That is, if I could find the right moment.

As the train rocked along, I also thought of Becca. I remembered how she'd looked at me with big, sad eyes as I said good-bye. I knew she'd survive the weekend, but I couldn't help worrying about her just a little. After all, she's only eight. It's hard to be apart from your family when you're that age.

Soon, though, I stopped worrying and started to feel excited. I noticed that the landscape we were passing through had changed. Instead of fields and woods and the occasional neighborhood, I was starting to see bigger buildings and busier roads. We were getting close to New York!

CHAPTER 4

Half an hour later, we had arrived in New York. We were whizzing along a crowded, traffic-filled street, stuffed into the back of a cab with Stacey's father. He'd met us at Grand Central Station and whisked us out onto the street and into the cab almost before I could catch my breath.

Manhattan. What an awesome place. I heard Stacey's dad ask about the train trip, but I let Stacey answer him. I was too busy staring out of the windows as the cab hurtled along. Why do cabs always drive so fast in New York? I guess they're just going with the flow. Everything is fast in the city. People talk fast, they walk fast, they do everything fast.

We stopped at a light, and hundreds of people streamed across the street. I saw men in business suits, carrying attaché cases. I saw women in business suits, carrying attaché cases and pocketbooks — and wearing running shoes instead of high heels. I saw women who looked like models, wearing amazingly chic outfits. Even Claud and Stacey don't dress like that! I saw bicycle messengers flying past, dodging people and cars. And I saw little old ladies carrying shopping bags and walking tiny dogs.

Everywhere I looked there was something to see, and I wanted to see it *all*, but I knew that if I looked in one direction I'd miss something in another. Stacey nudged me. "We're passing Bloomie's," she said.

I gaped at the big building with the brass-and-glass revolving doors, and at the sidewalk merchants who had set up tables in front of it.

"How about if we hop out and shop for a few minutes?" Stacey teased her dad. "You can wait in the cab."

He smiled. "I have other plans for you, young lady," he said. "I made dinner reservations at the Sign of the Dove."

"All *right*!" exclaimed Stacey. "My favorite."

For a minute I wished I could go with them. I love to eat out in fancy restaurants, and besides, I was still a little nervous about seeing — and having my Talk with — Quint. But then Mr. McGill asked, "What time are you due at your friend's house?", and I realized that I had to go through with my plans.

"Not until seven," I replied.

"Fine," he said. "Our reservation is for seven-thirty. We'll get you girls settled at my apartment, and then Stacey can put you in a cab."

Just then we pulled up in front of an old brick building. After Mr. McGill had paid the cab driver, we went inside and up to his apartment. I looked around. I'd been there before, but the last time I'd visited New York, I'd stayed at Laine Cummings' apartment, since I'd been traveling with the entire BSC and not all of us could fit into Mr. McGill's place. Laine Cummings used to be Stacey's best friend in New York, but they — well, they're not friends at all, anymore.

Anyway, Mr. McGill's apartment is nice. Kind of small, but nice. There are two bedrooms, one of which is for Stacey to use whenever she visits. The living room has brick walls and a fireplace, which I thought was pretty cool.

"You can stay in my room, with me," said Stacey. "I have a futon that unrolls into an extra bed." She showed me her room, and I stuck my overnight bag in a corner. Then I just stood for a moment with my hands in my pockets. I was feeling strange and out of place.

Stoneybrook is so small and quiet, and New York is so big and noisy. I was kind of overwhelmed.

"How about a soda?" asked Stacey. "We can relax for a few minutes before you have to go."

"Great," I said. I checked myself in the mirror that hung behind her door. "I don't think I'll change. Quint's family is pretty informal."

"You look fine," she assured me.

I smoothed my hair and followed her into the kitchen. We had sodas and talked to Mr. McGill for a little while, and then it was time for me to leave.

Stacey walked me downstairs and to the corner. "I'll get you a cab and give him Quint's address," she said. "When you get there, you pay him what it says on the meter, plus a tip, like fifteen percent."

I panicked. "How do I figure it out?" I asked.

"I usually just figure out what ten percent would be, like ten cents if it's a dollar. Then I add half again that much. So, like, another five cents would make fifteen cents, which is fifteen percent of a dollar. Get it?"

Math isn't my *strongest* subject, but I got the idea. I nodded.

"Then, when you're ready to leave, Quint

can put you in a cab back here. If you call me first I'll be waiting outside for you. Oh! There's a cab!" Stacey threw her arm up, and a cab veered out of the stream of traffic and stopped beside us. I was impressed. Stacey is so cool, she's chilly. (That's what my friends and I call anything that's mega-cool.)

I hopped in and Stacey gave the driver Quint's address. He pulled away before I even had time to say good-bye, so I just waved out the back window. As we drove along, I watched the scene on the street again, but I was a little distracted. It was getting awfully close to T-time: the time when I'd have my Talk with Quint. In my mind, so that the cab driver wouldn't think I was nuts, I started to rehearse the lines I'd worked out. "Quint," I'd say. "We need to talk. I like you a lot, and I'm glad we're friends, but — "

The cab screeched to a halt.

"What happened?" I asked.

"Isn't this the address your friend told me?" the driver asked.

I checked the building. "Oh, I guess it is," I said. I looked at the meter and was relieved to see a nice, even number. Six dollars. Ten percent of that would be sixty cents, and half again would make it ninety. I gave the driver seven dollars. "Keep the change," I said, feeling cosmopolitan and also a little pleased with my generosity, since I'd given him an extra dime.

"Thanks-have-a-nice-day," he droned, as if he said the same thing a thousand times a day and could hardly be bothered.

I stepped out, looked up at Quint's building, took a deep breath, and went inside.

The moment I saw Quint I felt less nervous. I really do like him a lot. He didn't kiss me or anything, either, which was a good thing since his little sister and brother, Morgan and Tyler, were standing right there. Morgan's six, and Tyler is nine. They would have teased the daylights out of us if Quint had acted like I was his girlfriend.

"Jessi," said Mrs. Walter, entering the room. "Nice to see you." She's soft-spoken and a little shy, but she seemed genuinely glad to see me. Quint's father came in, too. "Welcome," he said, smiling.

"Jessi! Jessi!" cried Morgan. "Watch what I can do!" She started to turn a cartwheel in the middle of the living room, which was not that huge. In fact, it's both the living room *and* the dining room; a big dining table is in the back, near the kitchen. "Uh, Morgan," I said. "That's nice, but — " I never know whether it's a good idea to tell kids what to do when their parents are standing right there. I mean,

I don't want to act as if I'm in *charge* or anything, but I *am* used to taking care of kids and I know that things like cartwheels in the living room aren't a great idea.

"Not here, honey," said Mrs. Walter, to my relief. "That's an outside trick."

Morgan looked pouty for a moment, but then she brightened. "I love your earrings," she said, looking at the fish-shaped silver ones I'd chosen to wear that night. "I have some jewelry in my room," she added, grabbing my hand. "Come on, I'll show you."

Tyler spoke up, too. "I have a new computer game," he said. "Want to see?"

I glanced at Quint, and he took over. "You guys," he said, "Jessi just got here. Anyway, I have something to show her, and she's *my* guest."

He led me to his room and showed me the program for his ballet recital. "Isn't this cool?" he said. "I feel like a real professional."

"I can't believe you almost didn't go to Juilliard," I said. Quint had had some doubts about being a dancer when I first met him. He loved ballet, but he *didn't* love all the teasing from boys who thought ballet was for sissies.

"I know," he replied. "It's the best thing that ever happened to me. And I owe it to you. You're the one who talked me into auditioning for the school." He smiled and leaned toward me with a look in his eyes that made me draw in my breath.

I was about to say, "Quint, we have to talk — "

But just then, Mrs. Walters called to say that dinner was ready. Saved by the bell.

The table was beautifully set, the chicken stew we had was great, and the conversation at dinner was fun, but I still felt just a little uncomfortable around Quint's family. I wanted them to like me, but I wasn't even sure whether I'd be having anything to do with Quint in the future. Maybe he'd hate me when I said what I had to say. Then his family would hate me, too. I tried to shrug off my nervousness, but it didn't go away entirely.

After dinner, Quint and I sat down in the TV room (which doubles as Mrs. Walters' study) to watch a Fred Astaire movie on the VCR. Tyler and Morgan followed us in, but the second they started to tease Quint about my being his girlfriend, he kicked them out. "We want to watch this movie in peace," he told his mother. "Isn't it their bedtime, anyway?"

We settled in, on opposite corners of the couch. Quint seemed a little shy — maybe because we hadn't seen each other in a while —

and I was glad. I tried to pay attention to the movie, but once again I was distracted by the idea of T-time drawing near. I peered over at Quint. He looked distracted, too. Then he grinned at me. "I'm really nervous about tomorrow night," he confessed. "It's an important performance."

That was it. I decided that T-time could wait until after the concert. I didn't want to upset Quint.

The movie ended, and we sat quietly for a while. I started to gaze out the window at the building next door, which was only about six feet away. It was kind of cool how you could see into other apartments. I saw a homey-looking kitchen, a starkly modern living room, and a playroom full of toys. Some apartments were so close that I could even hear snatches of conversation drifting across the airshaft. (Everybody's windows were open since it was a warm night.) "Great dinner, honey," said a man in a kitchen to his wife. "How about Mozart?" asked a woman standing by a hi-tech stereo in a modern living room.

One room was just opposite "my" window, but it was empty. It was a cozy-looking living room, with big over-stuffed sofas and chairs. I was just thinking how nice it looked when two men walked into the room. One of them sat down, and the other stood near him. Almost immediately, they started to talk in loud tones.

By now, Quint was looking over my shoulder. I guess we were being nosy *together*. We stared at the men, fascinated by being able to hear almost every word they said. Suddenly I turned to Quint. "Quint," I whispered, "I think they're *fighting*!"

CHAPTER 5

Within two seconds, there was no doubt about it. The men were fighting, and fighting very loudly. We probably could have heard them even if the windows had been closed.

The man who was sitting in the chair had red hair and a straggly beard and looked scary. The other man had thick, black hair and looked strong.

"You double-crossing weasel!" the black-haired man said.

"I'm not double-crossing you, Frank," replied the red-haired one. "It's just that I'm not so sure about this plan of yours."

"What are you talking about? We've worked on this plan for three months. It's foolproof, Red!"

Red shrugged. He looked sullen. "So you say, but I just don't know."

"What are you afraid of, you lily-livered,

chicken-hearted wimp?" asked Frank. "You make me sick!"

"I'm not afraid of anything — except getting busted."

"Busted?" roared Frank. "By the incompetent cops in this town? Forget it. This is the heist of the century. It'll go down in history as the perfect unsolved crime. The detectives will be going crazy, and we'll be in the islands, living the rest of our lives in luxury. Girls, rum, mangos, and papayas . . . "

I glanced at Quint and raised my eyebrows. Heist? Papayas? This was one of the most interesting — and confusing — conversations I'd ever heard. Not that I make a habit of eavesdropping. Quint looked back at me, and his eyes were big and round.

"I don't believe this," he whispered. "They're planning some kind of robbery, and we're hearing the whole thing. If they knew we were listening — " He looked scared, suddenly.

My mouth went dry. He was right to be scared. No crook likes to be overheard when he's planning a crime. In the movies, anybody who "knows too much gets killed." Without a word to each other, Quint and I simultaneously scooched down in our seats so that we couldn't be seen from the window. But there was no way we were about to stop listening.

The argument seemed to be gathering steam. "I've had it with you!" said Frank. "You may be an expert on jewels, but that's not enough. I need a partner who isn't going to wimp out on me."

"Just give me some time! These aren't just any jewels we're talking about, you know. The cops are going to go wild when this stuff turns up missing."

Jewels! This was getting better and better.

"I keep telling you," said Frank, "we don't need to worry about the cops. We'll be long gone before they even know the jewels are missing."

"I don't know," said Red again, looking stubborn. "Let's go over the plan one more time."

"*No!*" yelled Frank. "We've been over it a million times. You're either with me or *not* with me. And I gotta tell you, if you back out now, I'll kill you!"

Quint grabbed my arm, and I grabbed his. This was serious. I had no doubt that Frank meant what he said. He looked totally capable of killing somebody. He was tough and mean, and if I were Red I would run out of the room.

Just then, Quint's father cracked the door

to the TV room. "Quint! Jessi!" he called. "Turn down that TV! Morgan and Tyler are trying to get to sleep."

Quint and I looked at each other. My first impulse was to giggle. This was a real fight we were listening to, not the TV. We couldn't turn it down if we wanted to. But then I saw the panicked look in Quint's eyes, and I realized that this was no laughing matter. Quint's dad had just yelled out our names, loud enough for Frank and Red to hear. I turned to look out the window, and saw that the two of them had stopped arguing. Instead, they were staring across the airshaft — at us.

Quint jumped up and hit the light switch, and we were plunged into darkness. Then he grabbed me and pulled me to the floor. My elbow bumped against the couch on the way down, and it stung, but I was too scared to care. "What are you doing?" I hissed.

"I didn't want them to see us," he whispered back. "I had to move fast."

"Quint?" I said. "You *were* fast, but I don't think you were fast enough. I think they saw us."

He groaned. "They heard our names, too."

I lifted my head slowly so that I could peek out of the window again. If I saw Frank and Red staring back at me, I knew I would just die on the spot. But I didn't see them. In fact,

I couldn't see anything: they had pulled down the window blinds, and their apartment looked dark. "They're gone," I whispered to Quint. "Or at least, I can't see them anymore."

He stood up slowly and peeked across the way. Then, crouched down, he moved to the window and closed it. He scooted to the side of the window and pulled the cord that let the blinds down. Then he sat down next to me. He put his arm around me, and it felt good. I didn't think for a second about the Talk I'd wanted to have with him. I was feeling pretty shaky, and his arm was comforting. "Quint," I whispered, "we have to call the police."

He shook his head. "What would we tell them?" he asked. His voice sounded loud to me, and I tried to shush him. "It's okay," he said. "The window's closed." Quint seemed much calmer.

"We'd tell them that we witnessed two criminals planning a crime," I said, impatiently. I was still keeping my voice low.

"But we don't know *what* they were planning, or when it would happen," he said. "We don't have any real information at all. The police would probably just laugh at us. They'd think we were a couple of excited kids."

I started to argue, but I knew he was right. "But Quint," I said. "They saw us. They heard our names! And they know where you live."

He gave my shoulder a squeeze. "Don't worry," he said. "We'll probably never see them again. Do you know how many hundreds of people live just on this one block? I wouldn't know most of my neighbors if I tripped over them."

New York is so weird. I can't imagine not knowing my neighbors. But Quint sounded so sure of himself, and I wanted to believe him. "Maybe you're right," I said. "I mean, they probably didn't even think twice about a couple of kids overhearing their fight. Right?"

"Definitely." Quint *sounded* confident, but he didn't really look it. I could see doubt in his eyes. "Anyway, there's nothing we can do about it now."

"Quint," called Mrs. Walter. "I think it's about time for Jessi to go back to her friend's house. You need your rest tonight."

"Okay, Mom," replied Quint. "I guess she's right," he said to me. "I almost forgot to be nervous about my performance, after seeing *that*!" He gestured toward the window, then shook his head and grinned.

"Well, that's good, I guess. Anyway, you don't have to be nervous. You're going to be great."

"Listen," he said, ignoring my compliment. "Maybe we can spend some time tomorrow trying to find out more about those two guys.

Maybe if we got enough information, we *could* go to the police." He looked excited.

"I don't know. That could be dangerous."

"Not if we're careful. Come on. It'll be kind of fun. We can be detectives."

I felt like Red, arguing with Frank. I didn't want to be called a lily-livered chicken heart. "Well, okay," I said. I had a feeling that Quint was looking for something to take his mind off the dance concert. If we were *very* careful, playing detective might be just the thing. Anyway, the scene we'd witnessed was already beginning to seem unreal. Could we *really* have seen and heard two jewel thieves in the midst of planning a heist?

I called Stacey to let her know I was about to head back to her dad's apartment, and she agreed to meet me outside. Then, after I'd said good-bye to Mr. and Mrs. Walter and thanked them for dinner, Quint walked me downstairs.

"So you'll come over first thing tomorrow, right?" he was saying as we walked through the big door that led from the lobby to the street.

I was about to agree when I saw something that made me gasp. There, in front of Quint's building, stood Red and Frank. My heart started to pound, and I turned to Quint, speechless. He grabbed my arm and steered me past the men, down the block, and around the corner. I was sure the men were right behind us, but I was too afraid to look over my shoulder to check. So much for never seeing them again. I was terrified. They were following us already!

Quint hailed a cab that was speeding by. "Stacey's waiting for you," he said. "We'll talk tomorrow. There's no time now." He opened the door for me and I slid in, unable to say a word. "I can go into our building through the back way," he went on. "Don't worry about me." He gave the driver Stacey's address, called good night, and closed the door. The cab took off before I could say a thing.

I tried to compose myself as the cab sped toward Stacey's. I didn't want to seem upset in front of her, or even tell her about what had happened. I had the feeling that she might not like my playing detective, and I knew that since she was feeling responsible for me she would probably try to talk me out of it. On the other hand, I didn't feel I could back out on Quint now; we were in this together.

I was calmer by the time the cab pulled up in front of Stacey's building. In fact, I was able to act normal, and I don't think she noticed a thing. We headed up to the apartment, and I asked her if I could call Mallory to find out how Becca was doing.

"Sure," she said. "Dad and I are going to

be in the living room, watching a movie. You can use the phone in the kitchen."

I *did* want to ask Mal about Becca, but I was also dying to tell her what had happened that night. I knew she'd be fascinated. I dashed into the kitchen, grabbed the phone and dialed quickly. Mal answered. "It's me!" I cried, knowing she'd know who "me" was.

"Jessi!" she said. (See?) "How's New York?"

"You won't believe what happened," I replied. "But first, tell me how Becca's doing."

"Wellll . . . not so great, actually. She's having a tough time." Mal sounded pretty serious, so I sat down and got ready to listen. My news would have to wait.

Friday

This isn't an official BSC notebook entry, since I wasn't officially baby-sitting. I mean, my parents were both at home, so I wasn't actually responsible for all the kids. But I was in charge of Becca: Mom had asked me to make sure her visit with us went smoothly. Well, "smoothly" is not a word I would use to describe how Friday went. Words I might use instead are <u>disastrously</u>, <u>catastrophically</u>, <u>calamitously</u>. I'm using my thesaurus here, in case you can't tell. A writer has to have a good vocabulary. Anyway, as I was saying, Friday night with Becca did not go well.

Mal had reason to sound a little overwhelmed. She might have been exaggerating just a tiny bit — I mean, "calamitously?" — but from what I heard, Becca *was* quite a handful.

When I called her that night, she sounded as if she were about ready to hand in her Babysitter's License.

"Jessi," she said, "you know you're my best friend. And you know I love your family. But your little sister can be a — "

"A real pain," I said. "I know. I love her too, but I had a feeling this weekend wasn't going to be easy for you."

"I really feel sorry for her," said Mal. "I mean, she does feel awful and lonely and abandoned. But what can I do? I've made everything as nice as possible for her, but I can't make you and your family appear out of thin air."

"I know," I said. "But we'll be back soon. I guess that's what you have to keep telling her."

"It doesn't do any good," said Mallory, sighing. "She wouldn't eat dinner tonight, and she wouldn't play with the other kids *after* dinner, and now she says she can't sleep."

"No dinner?" I asked. I was surprised. Becca usually has a good appetite.

"Well, she did manage to swallow some of the chocolate pudding we had for dessert," admitted Mal. "Once I coaxed her into it." She giggled a little. "Now, if only I could get her to sleep — "

"Try *Charlotte's Web*," I suggested. "Read a chapter aloud to her. That always works." I spoke quickly. I was a little impatient with all this talk about Becca. I mean, I did care how she was doing, but I had more important things on my mind. It was time to change the subject. "Mal," I said, "listen to what happened." I told her what Quint and I had seen and heard. I didn't leave out any details, either. It made a good story.

"Wow," breathed Mal when I'd finished. "This is awesome! You actually saw two guys planning a jewel heist. I can't believe it."

"Me neither," I said. "But it really happened. It's just like a movie, isn't it?"

"Yeah," answered Mal. "Except for one thing. When you watch a movie, you get to go home later on and forget about it. But this is as if you and Quint are *in* the movie! Jessi, those guys might be after you. What are you going to do?"

I heard the fear in Mal's voice, and somehow it made me want to pretend I wasn't scared at all. "We're going to crack the case, that's what we're going to do. We'll take care of the thieves before they can do anything to us. All we need is a little concrete evidence, and then the police can take it from there." I sounded so confident that I almost convinced *myself*.

"Well," replied Mal, "all I can say is good luck. And be careful! Those guys could be dangerous." She paused for a second. "Jessi?" she said. "Becca's calling me. She's supposed to be sleeping on a cot in Vanessa's and my room, but she's saying she can't get to sleep. I better go."

"Okay. Good luck, yourself. Remember, *Charlotte's Web* usually does the trick. Try the chapter where Wilbur first meets Charlotte."

Mal told me later that her conversation with me was a real bright spot in her evening. It was good, she said, to talk over the "Becca problem" with someone who knew Becca well. It was also good to be distracted by my news about the jewel thieves. Ever since I'd left, Mal had been thinking about nothing but Becca and her needs, and she was beginning to get tired of the subject. Especially since, no matter what Mal did, Becca refused to cheer up.

This had started as soon as I'd left Becca in the Pikes' driveway. As I'd walked toward Stacey's house, Mal had taken Becca's hand. "Come on, Becca," she'd said. "Let's go inside and drop off your bag. Then we can join the scavenger hunt. Everyone's waiting for us!"

"No," said Becca. She put her duffel bag down on the driveway and sat on it. "I'm staying right here until my family comes back."

Mal almost giggled, but she managed not to. "Becca," she said. "You can't do that. It's going to get chilly when the sun goes down. And besides, you'll want dinner and a bed later on."

"Will not," said Becca. "I'm an orphan, and orphans don't need anything from anybody."

"You're not an orphan," said Mal patiently. "Your family will come back soon, and meanwhile you're an honorary member of *my* family. And even orphans need to eat and sleep and — get hugs." Mal reached down as she spoke and gave Becca an especially nice hug. Becca burst into tears. Mal squeezed her harder, and then gently helped her up and into the house.

Once Becca had been persuaded to part with her duffel bag (which wasn't easy), Mal rounded up the other kids and told them it was time for the scavenger hunt. "Becca and Claire will be one team," she said. "I'll help them until I have to go to the Baby-sitters Club meeting."

Claire jumped up and down. "Yea!" she said. "I get to be on Becca-silly-billy-goo-goo's team!'' Claire is five, and she can be pretty silly sometimes.

"Vanessa and Nicky and Margo will be another team,'' Mal went on.

"I have to be with two girls?'' asked Nicky. "Ew!'' Nicky's eight, and like most eight-year-olds, he pretends that girls are poison. In reality, he loves his sisters and likes the attention he gets from them. Vanessa is nine, and she's kind of dreamy. She wants to be a poet when she grows up. Margo, who's seven, is much more practical than Vanessa. In fact, at times she likes to try to run the Pike household. She's been in a bossy phase lately.

"And the triplets will be the last team,'' Mal went on. She would have liked to separate the triplets and put them on different teams, but she knew they wouldn't stand for it. Jordan, Adam, and Byron, who are ten, stick together like glue. They're identical in looks only, though. Adam and Jordan are both crazy about sports, while Byron is more quiet and sensitive. Jordan takes piano lessons. Adam wants to learn how to scuba dive someday. The triplets can be a handful, but that day they were no match for Becca.

"I don't *wanna* go on a scabenger hunt,'' said Becca as soon as Mal had finished making up the teams.

"It's *scavenger* hunt,'' said Mal. "And I bet

you don't even know what one is. It'll be fun, I promise. See, what we have to do is find the things on these lists. The first team to find all their items wins." Mal had made up three lists, with pretty simple things on them. This was going to be a short scavenger hunt.

She passed out the lists. "Oh, no," said Margo, looking at her team's list. "Where are we going to find a feather duster?"

"I know!" said Nicky. He put his head next to Margo's and started to whisper excitedly. The scavenger hunt was on.

Mal said Becca followed her around the way a puppy follows its mother. She showed no interest in the scavenger hunt; all she wanted was for Mal to pay attention to her. Mal tried to involve her in the game. "Becca," she said, "where to you think we might find a red sock?"

"I dunno," Becca replied. "When do you think my mom will call?"

Mal rolled her eyes, without letting Becca see. "She said she'd call after dinner," she told her, for what felt like the millionth time. "How about helping us find some things now? It'll keep your mind off missing your family."

"My family!" Becca wailed. "They don't love me. Nobody loves me. I'm all alone." Becca was, at the moment she said that, surrounded by Pike kids. Almost everyone was in the kitchen, looking for things like egg timers, bottle caps, and toothpicks.

"You're not alone, Becca," said Claire helpfully. "You're with us!"

"You're with us, and we're with you, next time maybe we'll go to the zoo," Vanessa rhymed. Becca didn't crack a smile.

The scavenger hunt finished up right around dinnertime, just as Mal returned from the BSC meeting. The triplets won by a mile. They'd been able to talk Mrs. Pike into giving them the shoelaces out of her favorite sneakers. That item had completed their list. Mal gave them each a quarter for a prize.

Dinner in the Pike household is never boring. Mr. and Mrs. Pike don't believe in fighting with the kids over what they eat. There's always plenty of food on the table, of all different kinds. That night, for example, the triplets were eating make-it-yourself tacos, Vanessa and Claire were eating the taco filling over rice, Margo was having a peanut-butter-and-banana sandwich (the only thing she eats these days, according to Mal), and Nicky was just eating taco shells with nothing in them.

Becca wasn't eating at all. She sat at the

table with her hands folded in her lap, doing her best to look like a pathetic, unloved orphan.

"Becca," Mal said, "does anything here look good?" She happens to know that Becca loves tacos.

"I'm not hungry," said Becca.

Mal tried to tempt Becca with whatever food she could find in the kitchen, but Becca refused it all. (Except for the chocolate pudding, I guess.)

After dinner, Mal told Becca she could watch TV with the others for an hour, and then it would be time for bed. Becca sat in the corner of the couch, as far away from everyone else as she could get, and pulled a pillow over her stomach. When the phone rang, though, she jumped up, smiling. "That's my mom!" she said, looking happy for the first time all day. Luckily, she was right.

Becca seemed better after the phone call, but Mal still had a hard time getting her into her pajamas. "I'm not going to sleep, so why should I put on my pajamas?" asked Becca logically. Finally Mal coaxed Becca into bed, and that's when I called.

After she hung up with me, Mal returned to her bedroom. She didn't tell Becca that I'd called, since she didn't want to excite her. It was getting late. Instead, she pulled her well-worn copy of *Charlotte's Web* from the shelf, and began to read. Becca listened intently for a while, but her eyelids began to droop before Mal was even halfway through the chapter. Like I said, it always works!

CHAPTER 7

"Beep, beep, beep, CRASH!" I heard the noises from the street below. Stacey had told me I'd probably be wakened up by the sound of garbage trucks backing up (that was the "beep, beep, beep" sound) and by the noise of cans being thrown into the backs of the trucks (that was the "CRASH"). She was right about the noises, but she wasn't right about their waking me up. According to the clock on Stacey's night table, it was only six in the morning, but already I felt as if I'd been up for hours. I hadn't slept well at all.

It wasn't that I was uncomfortable on the futon, or that I was nervous about being in the city. It was that I couldn't stop thinking about what Quint and I had seen and heard. Jewel thieves! Mean, nasty jewel thieves. Mean, nasty jewel thieves who *knew my name*!

They knew what I looked like, too. And they'd probably seen me leaving Quint's building. I wondered whether they could have followed us and seen me getting into a cab. They might even have gotten into a cab of their own and followed me all the way to Mr. McGill's building! I wondered if they were waiting for me downstairs.

I tossed and turned for awhile, trying to fall asleep again. Finally I gave up and just lay there, thinking. Or maybe worrying is a better word. I knew I'd feel better as soon as I was with Quint again and we started to do some detective work — *doing* is always better than worrying. But it was too early to get up. I didn't want to wake Stacey, and I knew Quint's family wouldn't be expecting visitors until later on.

I rolled over and grabbed the book I'd brought. It was *Misty of Chincoteague*, which I have read probably five hundred times. There's something wonderful about re-reading a favorite book. It's just so comforting to follow the familiar words and to watch the plot unfold in the way you know it will. Before long I was swept up in the story, and my worries dropped away.

"Morning, Jessi," said Stacey, sleepily. It was about eight by the time she rolled over and rubbed her eyes. "Sleep well?"

"Sure," I lied.

"Ready for breakfast? I bet Dad has bagels

and cream cheese and stuff. He always goes to Zabar's to stock up before I visit." Zabar's is this huge food store on the other side of town, near where Quint lives. It sells all kinds of great stuff.

"I'm starved," I replied. I was, too. I guess lying awake for hours can really build up your appetite.

I dressed in my "walking around the city" outfit, and joined Stacey and her dad for breakfast. Stacey was right. Mr. McGill *had* gone to Zabar's, and he'd gotten tons of food. I don't usually eat big breakfasts because I have to keep in shape for ballet. But that morning, I ate until I was stuffed. I figured I'd need my energy. You'd think that being nervous would affect my appetite, but no. I'm hungry no matter what kind of mood I'm in.

As soon as we had finished eating, Stacey took me downstairs to hail a cab. She knew I was in a hurry to get to Quint's. "My father wants to take us all out to lunch today," she told me. "You, me, and Quint. So give us a call in a few hours and we'll figure out where to meet, okay?"

"Great," I said. "That's really nice of your dad." We were about to walk out of the building at that point, and I was a little distracted. I peered around, checking to make sure the two men weren't lurking nearby.

"What are you looking for?" asked Stacey.

"Oh, um, a cab," I said, thinking quickly.

"We'll have a better chance out on the avenue." Stacey led me to the corner where we'd stood the night before. "Why don't *you* try hailing one this time?" she asked.

I watched for a cab, and when I saw one coming I threw my arm up, just as I'd seen Stacey and Quint do. It worked! The cab veered over to me and pulled up at the curb. It was almost like magic. Stacey grinned at me. "You're a New Yorker already," she said. "See you later!"

I spent the cab ride thinking about — what else? — the jewel thieves. And when I jumped out at Quint's, guess what I saw? A police car, parked in the street in front of the building next door. The building where *they* had been having their argument!

"It's been there all morning," whispered Quint, when I mentioned it to him. He and I had escaped from his family as quickly as possible and were alone in the TV room.

"Maybe the police are already on to those guys," I said. "Maybe they're staking out the apartment."

"Maybe," said Quint, sounding doubtful. "Listen to this, though," he went on. "My dad told me at breakfast this morning that the phone rang in the middle of the night. When he picked it up, whoever was on the other end hung up. It happened twice!"

A shiver ran down my spine. "Do you think they were calling to check up on you?" I asked.

He shrugged. "Who knows? It could have been just a coincidence. Anyway, should we check up on *them*?" He gestured toward the window.

"I — I don't know. This is making me nervous."

"I'm kind of nervous about it, too. In fact, I didn't sleep very well last night. But wouldn't we feel better if we were *doing* something?"

I guess this is why Quint and I are friends: we really are a lot alike.

"That's exactly what I was thinking," I said. So we walked over to the window and peeked through the blinds. Our window was open, and so were most of the ones across the way, including the one we were most interested in. But nobody was in sight. I started to turn away when suddenly I heard a familiar voice.

"Listen, numbskull," it said.

"That's him," hissed Quint. "They must be in another room."

We strained to hear the conversation.

"We're almost ready for this job," the voice went on. I recognized it as Frank's. "We could even do it tomorrow. But there are still a couple of details to take care of, and I need your help. So are you in? Or are you out?"

It was the same argument they'd been having the night before.

"I'm in, I'm in," said Red. "You talked me into it."

I guess "If you back out now, I'll kill you" is a pretty persuasive argument.

"All right then," said Frank. "Let's get going."

Quint and I looked at each other with raised eyebrows. "Come on," he said. On our way out of the apartment, Quint called out to his mother. "We're going out for awhile. See you later!"

"Just be sure you're back from your lunch by two o'clock," she answered. Quint had a rehearsal that afternoon in preparation for the evening performance. His parents were going out with friends at the same time, so Stacey and I had volunteered to baby-sit for Morgan and Tyler.

We ran out of Quint's building just as Red and Frank were emerging from theirs. "Whoa, get back," whispered Quint. "Let's see where they're going." We watched intently as the men walked up the block and then crossed the street. "Looks like they're headed for the park," Quint said. "Let's go."

I noticed that the police car had disappeared. Most likely, it had been there for some other reason. In any case, no police were following Red and Frank. It was up to us now. We headed up the block, sticking close to the buildings so that the thieves wouldn't see us if they turned around. Then we crossed into the park, as they had.

Central Park is a pretty amazing place. It's not just trees and grass. It's chock full of roller-skaters and joggers and bikers. Also kite-flyers, baby-stroller pushers, dog-walkers, and softball-players. Also — well, I could go on forever. Let's just say a lot of people are doing a lot of different things. Also, there are all these neat things to see, like the very place where we were entering the park. We walked beneath this big arbor, with trailing vines all over it. It was like walking into a fairy tale. And then there's Strawberry Fields. What is that? Well, it's a memorial for John Lennon. You know, the Beatle who died? People come from all over to see it. Part of it is this design in black-and-white stone that says "Imagine" in the middle of it. I was almost distracted by that, but Quint pulled on my arm. "Come on," he said. "We're going to lose them if we're not careful."

Luckily, Red's outstanding feature (his hair!) made him easy to spot. And since we were in the park, it wasn't hard to stay close behind him and Frank and still stay hidden by trees and shrubs.

We were so close to them, in fact, that we could pick up bits of conversation now and then. We heard Red ask Frank if he had a cigarette. We heard Frank tell Red it was supposed to rain the next day. And we heard them talking about the Palm Court, which Quint told me is a restaurant at the Plaza Hotel.

They crossed the drive, where traffic goes through the park, and so did we. They kept walking, and soon we all emerged near a fountain. "Bethesda Terrace," said Quint. "This is a neat place to hang out on a sunny day."

I saw a lake nearby, with rowboats on it. Red and Frank headed toward it. "I wonder if they're going to go for a row!" I said, giggling. I wasn't feeling so nervous anymore. In fact, I was kind of enjoying myself.

"Stay close," said Quint. "We don't want to lose them if they go into the boathouse." He pointed to a building. "That's where you can rent boats. They also have bikes you can rent. Plus a cafe."

Next, we followed Red and Frank past the little pond where people sail their model sailboats. I remembered it from other visits. "There's the Alice statue," I said, pointing. I gazed at the giant statue of Alice in Wonderland. Every time I've seen it kids have been climbing all over it. That day was no exception.

"Watch out!" cried Quint. "They're getting ready to leave the park, I think. Hmmm, Seventy-ninth Street. Wonder where they're headed."

I was a little sorry to leave the park. I think it's my favorite place in New York, next to Lincoln Center, that is.

"Aha!" said Quint, after a few minutes. "They're going into the museum."

We stood for a moment and watched as Red and Frank climbed the big stone steps of the Metropolitan Museum of Art. It's a huge building, and it looks incredibly impressive, but also kind of friendly. Why friendly? Well, for one thing, these colorful banners hang from the front. They put them up to announce special shows. Also, the steps are full of people who are waiting for friends, eating pretzels they've bought from vendors on the sidewalk, or just sitting in the sun. It looks like a fair or something.

We raced up the stairs behind Frank and Red, and into the dark, cool entrance. "Wow!" I said, looking around. We were in a huge, cavernous hall.

"Darn," said Quint.

"What?" I asked.

"I don't have any extra money — not if we want to take a cab when we go to lunch. Do you have any?" He pointed to a sign that said, "Pay what you wish, but you must pay something."

"Nope," I said. "Nothing extra. I guess that's the end of the line. We can't follow them any further." We watched as Red and Frank disappeared into the crowd. "I wonder what they came here for, anyway," I said, as we walked back outside.

"Jessi, do you think — " Quint said, in an awed voice. He was pointing to a red and orange banner that said, "Coming Soon: Jewels of the Russian Empire."

I stared at it, open-mouthed. Could Red and Frank actually be planning to rob the Metropolitan Museum? Suddenly I realized I might be in over my head.

CHAPTER 8

After Quint and I had gazed at the banner for a moment or two, we walked down the steps to the sidewalk. "Can we rest for a few minutes?" I asked. "I'm feeling a little overwhelmed."

"Sure," Quint said. He led me past the museum. "How about here, near the temple? We can sit on the grass."

I studied the huge glass structure that loomed over us. It looked like a giant greenhouse, but inside, instead of plants, was a temple! That's right, an entire Egyptian temple that was brought over and set up inside its own wing attached to the museum. It's made of big tan-colored stones, and looks incredibly old. It is the coolest thing I've ever seen. It took my mind off Frank and Red, for a few minutes at least.

"There's still nothing we can do," said Quint, as if he'd been thinking the situation over. "I mean, we can't walk in and tell the guards that someone is planning to steal the Russian jewels. They wouldn't believe us, and why should they? We have no proof. It's just a guess."

I shook my head. "I know. We're really stuck. We can't go to the police until we have more to tell them, but the longer we wait, the better the chances are that Frank and Red will steal the jewels."

"We'll just have to stay on our toes," said Quint. "And we can't forget that they know our names. They could be watching out for us, just like we're watching out for them."

I hadn't forgotten, not for one minute. The only reason I'd been able to enjoy following those crooks through the park was because we had been behind them. For once, I didn't have to worry about *them* being behind *me*.

"Hey, aren't we supposed to meet Stacey and her dad for lunch?" asked Quint, looking at his watch. "It's almost noon. We should call them."

We stood up and headed for a phone booth. I dialed Mr. McGill's number, and Stacey answered right away. "Hi!" I said. "Are we still meeting you for lunch?"

"Definitely," replied Stacey. "We've been shopping all morning, and I'm starved."

"Where should we meet you?" I asked.

"It's up to you and Quint. Wherever you guys would like to go is fine with us."

I covered the mouthpiece with my hand for a second and looked at Quint. "It's up to us where we go," I told him.

His eyes lit up and I knew what he was thinking. "The Palm Court," he said.

I nodded. "Could we go to the Palm Court?" I asked Stacey.

"Sure," she said, sounding a little surprised.

"I always wanted to see the Plaza," I went on, hoping to explain my choice.

"Sounds like fun. Can you meet us there at twelve-thirty?"

I checked with Quint, and he nodded. "We'll be there," I said. I hung up.

Quint checked his watch again. "If we take a cab, we'll be there in no time," he said. "We can hang out here for a little longer and see if the men come out of the museum."

We picked out a place on the steps in front of the museum and settled in. All around us, people were eating lunch, talking, playing patty-cake with their babies, and reading. I've noticed that New Yorkers have an ability to make themselves comfortable wherever they are. One woman was even holding up a reflective tanning mirror to her face. I was so involved in my people-watching that I forgot to Frank-and-Red-watch, but luckily Quint

74

wasn't as distractable as me. He kept an eagle eye on the entrance.

"Is that them?" he asked, at one point. He jumped up and shaded his eyes, trying to get a better look. I jumped up, too, but all I saw was a skinny girl with short red hair. We sat down again. The sun felt good on my shoulders, and it had warmed the stone steps. I leaned back and closed my eyes, feeling very sleepy all of a sudden.

"Jessi, wake up!" cried Quint, shaking me. "We better get going or we'll be late for lunch."

"I wasn't asleep," I protested. But I rubbed my eyes and yawned. Maybe I *had* drifted off for a few seconds. After all, I'd barely slept the night before. It wasn't surprising that I was tired. "Did they come out?" I asked.

Quint shook his head, looking disgusted. "No," he replied. "It looks like we've lost them for the day. Unless they turn up at the Palm Court."

"Let's go," I said. "Maybe they're there already."

We walked down to the street, and Quint stepped forward to look for a cab. I pulled his arm. "I can do it," I said. "Check this out." I looked up the street until I saw a cab coming, and then I threw up my arm. The cab pulled over, and I opened the door for a surprised-looking Quint. I slid in behind him. "The Plaza, please," I said to the driver. I was tempted to add, "And make it snappy," like they do in the movies, but I was afraid it might sound rude. Besides, we weren't in *that* much of a hurry.

Quint gave me a grin and held up his hand for a high-five. "All *right*, Jessi," he said. "Very cool."

We arrived at the Plaza right on time. Quint led the way through the hotel's lobby, which was full of very rich-looking ladies with fancy luggage. Just seconds ago, in the cab, I'd been feeling very sophisticated. But now, suddenly, I felt like a hick. I gazed around, noticing the beautiful furniture, the heavy drapes, the thick carpets. Then I looked down at myself and realized that I was most definitely *not* dressed for the Plaza. I hadn't seen too many other people in jeans. I felt kind of shy and embarrassed. Then Quint tugged on my arm.

"Look," he said. "Does she look familiar?" He pointed to a portrait of a spunky-looking little girl.

"Eloise!" I said. "That was my favorite book when I was little." I walked closer to the picture. It was signed by the artist, Hilary Knight. "This is great," I said. "It's like Eloise was real." The book is about this little girl who lives at the Plaza and gets into all kinds of mischief. It's really funny.

"There's the Palm Court," said Quint, pointing. I pulled myself away from Eloise and followed him toward the restaurant. When we reached the entrance, this man in a tuxedo stopped us.

"Can I help you?" he asked, sounding rather snooty. He obviously couldn't figure out what two kids like us were doing at such a fancy restaurant.

Quint impressed me by acting extremely cool and mature. "We're meeting some friends," he said. "They may have already arrived. It's the McGill party."

"Ah, the McGill party," said the man. "Right this way, sir." He led us through the restaurant to a table where Stacey and her father were waiting. Then he pulled out a chair for me and gave Quint a slight bow.

"Thank you," said Quint and I at the same time.

"Hi, Jessi," said Stacey. "Isn't this place elegant?" She smoothed the pink tablecloth in front of her.

I looked around. I hadn't even been paying attention to the decor. When we walked through the restaurant, I'd been looking around at the people, checking to see if Frank and Red were there. I had a feeling Quint had done the same thing. In the cab, we'd discussed what we would do if we saw them. Our plan was to a) alert the police immediately if the two of them did anything at all suspicious, or b) make a run for it if they seemed to recognize us.

I had noticed that most of the people eating at the Palm Court looked very wealthy. In fact, many of the women were wearing jewels! I'd never seen so many diamond rings, pearl necklaces, and emerald earrings in my life. I wondered if Frank and Red might be planning a daring midday hold-up in the middle of the Palm Court. Now *that* would be exciting.

"Jessi!" Stacey was giving me a funny look. "What *are* you thinking about? You're acting like you're lost in space."

"More like 'out to lunch,' " cracked Quint. Everybody laughed, even Mr. McGill.

Just then, a waiter came by. He was wearing forest-green pants, a starched white jacket, and a mustard-colored sash. I made sure to take note of his outfit, so I could tell Claudia about it. It was a pretty cool uniform. "Would you care to order?" he asked.

"We need just a few minutes," said Mr. McGill. The waiter nodded and disappeared.

I looked at the menu in front of me, wondering what kind of exotic food might be served at a place like this. It turned out to be a pretty regular menu. There were things like club sandwiches, chicken salad, and seafood salad.

"Let's get the tea sandwiches," said Stacey. "They're always fun."

"Fine," I said. I was still thinking about Frank and Red, and I was a little too nervous to concentrate on the menu.

Quint and I kept glancing around surreptitiously, but Frank and Red did not appear. Finally, when the sandwiches arrived, I decided to forget about the jewel thieves and pay attention to my lunch at the fabulous Palm Court. Just as I was biting into a cucumber-and-watercress sandwich (with the crusts cut off — very fancy), I heard a lovely sound. "What's that?" I asked.

"Harp music," said Stacey. "A harpist plays here every day at lunch."

I looked around and saw the harpist. "Wow," I said. "Awesome." And finally I forgot about Frank and Red and just enjoyed the feeling of "dining out in style." Quint seemed to enjoy himself, too, although I'm not sure he was crazy about the tea sandwiches. The tiny squares of banana bread with pink cream cheese did not exactly make a hearty lunch, and he looked a little silly trying to eat them delicately. I had a feeling he'd much rather have ordered a cheeseburger and fries.

By the end of the meal, Frank and Red had not shown up, but I didn't care. I was going to be able to go back to Stoneybrook and tell everyone that I'd eaten lunch at the Plaza.

CHAPTER 9

"Thank you, Mr. McGill," I said. "That was a wonderful lunch."

"Thanks, Dad," chimed in Stacey.

"Thanks a lot," added Quint.

Stacey's father had signalled for the check and the waiter had brought it in a leather folder. Mr. McGill counted out bills and tucked them inside. "Well," he said, "I'm glad you enjoyed it. I wasn't sure you'd think the harp music and the little sandwiches were cool, but I guess if you wanted cool you'd have chosen the Hard Rock Cafe."

"That's right," said Stacey. "This time we were going for elegance, instead. Right, Jessi?"

"Right," I answered, feeling guilty. I hadn't been thinking about elegance when I chose the Palm Court. I'd been thinking about jewel thieves. I felt bad about hiding the truth from Stacey, but I still thought it would be a bad idea to tell her about our mystery. After all,

Quint and I had things under control. If I told Stacey what was going on, she'd probably send me back to Stoneybrook.

"Okay, kiddo," said Mr. McGill to Stacey. "I'm off to the salt mines. Have fun baby-sitting. We'll have dinner together, okay?"

Stacey nodded. I could tell she was mad that her father was going to his office while she was visiting for the weekend, but she was trying not to show it. Stacey's dad is kind of a workaholic, and I know that bothers her. He just never seems to stop working, and he doesn't have a lot of energy left over to spend on his family. In fact, from what Stacey's told me, his work habits were part of the reason for her parents' divorce.

We walked out of the restaurant together. Stacey's dad hugged her and gave her some money. "Why don't you kids take a cab up to Quint's?" he said.

We thanked him again and said our good-byes. I turned to check the entrance to the Plaza one more time, looking for Frank and Red, and by the time I turned around Stacey had hailed a cab.

We reached Quint's just in time. Mr. and Mrs. Walter were dressed and ready to go out, and Quint had to leave for his dress rehearsal. "We really appreciate your taking care of Morgan and Tyler," Mrs. Walter said to Stacey and me. "I know you baby-sit at home all the time, so it's nice of you to work while you're on vacation."

"That's okay," said Stacey. "We love to sit, and it's always fun to do things in the city with kids."

"Anyway," I added, "Morgan and Tyler are great kids. It'll be a pleasure to take care of them."

Quint rolled his eyes. "You can't be talking about Morgan and Tyler *Walter!*" he said. "The pests of the universe!"

Morgan and Tyler jumped on him and pulled at his shirt. "We are not!" cried Morgan.

"*You're* a pest," yelled Tyler. "*You* are!"

"Okay, okay," said Quint, grinning. "I'm a pest, and you guys are perfect. Is that better?"

"Yeah!" said Tyler and Morgan.

After a few minutes, Quint and his parents said good-bye and left Stacey and me alone with Morgan and Tyler. "How about a trip to the zoo, you guys?" asked Stacey. She and I had already planned to take the kids there, since we both love zoos.

"All *right!*" said Tyler

"Will we see the monkeys?" asked Morgan.

"Absolutely," said Stacey. She and I helped the kids find their jackets, and then we set off. Stacey led us down Central Park West to a park entrance near Tavern on the Green, which is this really fancy restaurant.

I was taking my second walk through the park in one day, but I didn't mind. There's so much to see in Central Park. I bet you could walk through it every single day and see new things each time. But even though the park is beautiful and full of interesting people and places, I couldn't totally relax and enjoy it. I was nervous about being out in the city without Quint. What if Frank and Red had watched Stacey and me and the kids leave the Walters' apartment? What if they were following us? I could be putting Morgan and Tyler in danger. I kept glancing over my shoulder, checking to make sure the two men weren't behind me.

Luckily, we were walking through this huge field called the Sheep Meadow, and there wasn't much cover for Frank and Red to duck behind if they *were* following us. I was able to rest easy for a few minutes and watch the people who were flying kites and playing softball.

After a while, we walked under a big arch. "That's Playmates Arch," said Stacey. "It's called that because it leads to the playing fields."

All of a sudden, Morgan grabbed my hand. "Jessi!" she said. I jumped, since I was feeling jittery to begin with.

"What?" I asked. "What's the matter?"

"I hear the carousel," she said. "Can we go on it?"

I calmed down. "Sure," I replied, digging into my pockets for change. "Let's go buy tickets for you and Tyler."

"I don't want to go on the dumb carousel," said Tyler. "That's for little kids."

Stacey and I grinned at each other, remembering a time when the entire BSC had visited New York. We had fallen under the spell of the carousel, and we had a great time riding on it. "*I'll* go with you, Morgan," I said.

"Me, too," said Stacey.

Tyler looked at us. "*You're* going on it?" he asked. "Well, I guess I might as well, too." He looked happy, even though he was trying to sound bored and sophisticated. And when we climbed onto the merry-go-round's horses, which are almost as big as real horses, his face lit up and he looked as excited as any other kid on the ride.

I chose a white stallion with a purple-and-red saddle, trimmed in gold. And during the ride, I happily pretended he was real. I even gave him a name: Charger. I love horses, all horses. Even the ones carved out of wood.

But when the carousel stopped and we hopped off, reality came flooding back. I was not a beautiful damsel with her own white stallion. I was Jessi, in the big city, mixed up with a pair of jewel thieves. I followed Stacey as she led us toward the zoo, but I started to glance behind me again, every few steps.

"There's the dairy," said Stacey. "In the olden days cows really got milked in there. Isn't it awesome to think that this spot — where we're standing right now — used to be the country?"

"Yeah," I replied, distractedly.

"Jessi," said Stacey, looking at me closely, "are you feeling all right?"

"I'm fine," I said. Just then I caught a glimpse of red over Stacey's shoulder, and my eyes widened. Was it Red? No, it was just a balloon, bobbing along over a baby stroller.

"What's the matter, Jessi?" Stacey asked.

At that moment, I wanted to tell her everything. I just couldn't keep the mystery a secret any longer. "I'll tell you," I said. "But let's get to the zoo, first. I don't want the kids to hear this."

We were passing under the Delacorte Clock then, and Tyler and Morgan were gazing up at it, hoping to see the animal band. That clock is so neat. Every half hour, this mechanical six-piece animal band circles around while it plays a tune. Plus, there are two monkeys on the top that bang little hammers on the bells.

Several minutes later, we arrived at the zoo.

Stacey had been giving me curious looks, but she hadn't asked any more questions. She was waiting patiently for me to explain why I'd been acting so weird.

The Central Park Zoo re-opened recently after being closed for a long time while the city fixed it up. It's a neat place to take kids to, since it's not all that big. Stacey told me that you can see all the animals in about an hour. We brought Morgan and Tyler straight to the Sea Lion pool, and they ran to the railing and started to make up names for each sea lion. "That one's Waldo," cried Morgan.

"And his wife Winifred," added Tyler.

Stacey and I sat down on a nearby bench so we could talk and watch the kids at the same time. "Okay," she said. "What's going on?"

It all came flooding out. I told her everything, starting with the fight Quint and I had seen the night before. Well, I told her almost everything. I couldn't quite bring myself to admit why I'd wanted to go to the Palm Court.

Stacey gazed at me, wide-eyed. "Wow," she said. "Jewel thieves!"

I'd expected her to be mad at me for getting involved, but she seemed more interested than mad. She asked me about every detail, and wondered out loud what Frank and Red might be planning. I should have remembered that every member of the BSC *loves* mysteries!

Morgan and Tyler finally tired of the sea lions, so we walked around the rest of the zoo. We saw the monkeys, which live in the Temperate Territory, and we visited the Tropic Zone, which is like a miniature rain forest. My favorite spot was the Polar Circle, with its huge penguin tank and a polar bear floe.

By the time we had seen everything in the zoo, we were exhausted. We decided to take a cab back to the Walters', which meant we would be the first ones home.

"The light's blinking!" yelled Tyler as soon as we walked into the apartment. He rushed over to the answering machine that sat near the phone. "I want to listen to the messages," he said.

Stacey and I looked at each other and shrugged. "Okay," I said. "Go ahead."

He punched a button and I heard the tape rewind. "Beep," said the machine. Then I heard Stacey's father's voice. "This is a message for Stacey," he said. "It's three-thirty, and I'm leaving the office now. I'll be home by the time you get there. See you, boontsie!"

Stacey blushed when she heard him call her by the nickname he gave her when she was a baby.

The machine beeped again, as if another message were coming up. But all I heard after that was a series of clicks. Tyler looked at me and shrugged, and I shrugged, too. But a moment later, when he and Morgan had gone into the kitchen to rummage for a snack, I turned to Stacey. "Do you think the phone has been tapped?" I asked. "I bet that's what those noises mean."

"You mean Frank and Red — " she began, but just then Mr. and Mrs. Walter came home, and Quint was a few seconds behind them. I didn't want to upset Quint right before his performance, so I didn't say a word about the phone. Anyway, Stacey and I had to head back to the East Side to change and get ready for a night out in the Big Apple!

CHAPTER 10

Sunday

If I hadent been reading the club notbook, I probibly woudent beleive that Becka was unhippy at first about being left at the Pikes. From what I culd see on Sunday, she was haveing a grate old time. She was ackting just like one of the fammily. And you shuld have seene what hapenned when her parrents came to pick her up.

I am very thankful to Mary Anne for the way she handled Becca that day. All of the BSC members are great sitters, but none of us is as sensitive as Mary Anne. She's the only one who could have helped Becca with what she was going through.

Mary Anne and Mal were sitting for all the Pike kids — plus Becca — on Saturday afternoon. (While I was running around in Central Park, they were running around the Pikes' backyard!) It was a beautiful day in Stoneybrook, and the Pike kids had spring fever. Everybody was outside in the yard.

The triplets and Nicky were throwing a softball around, playing "hot potato." In that game you have to catch the ball and then throw it again as soon as you can. The players stand in a circle, and the ball goes back and forth. There were wild throws now and then, and Mary Anne was keeping a close eye on the game to make sure none of the wild throws went anywhere near a window. The triplets have broken windows before, playing softball. The last time they did it they decided to keep quiet about which one of them had thrown the fateful ball. All three of them were grounded.

Claire and Margo were playing hopscotch on the driveway. They'd drawn a pattern in the shape of a seashell. "No fair!" yelled Claire, as Margo breezed through numbers one through five. "I only got to three!" Soon after, Margo touched the ground as she picked up her pebble, and Claire settled down and took her turn.

Vanessa was wandering among the tulips, composing an Ode to Spring. "How fair their little faces are, the flowers of the Spring," she muttered to herself, "turned up to catch the sunbeams that the elves and fairies bring." She smiled vaguely when Mal told her the poem sounded nice. Vanessa was off in her own little world.

Mal and Mary Anne sat on lawn chairs, with their own faces turned up to catch sunbeams. "Isn't it great to sit outside without even having to wear a sweat shirt?" asked Mal.

"It sure is," said Mary Anne. "Now all we have to put on is sunscreen." They'd made sure the kids were wearing some. Mary Anne glanced over toward the apple tree. Becca was sitting under it, looking forlorn. "How's Becca been doing?" she asked.

"Well, she's a *little* better," replied Mal. "She isn't crying all the time, and this morning she actually ate a bowl of cereal with strawberries on it. But she's still pretty unhappy. She keeps walking around with this 'poor little me' face on."

"I feel sorry for her," said Mary Anne. "I mean, not only is her whole family away, but Charlotte's away, too. And even though she's here with you guys, nobody can take the place of her family and her best friend."

"I know," said Mal with a sigh. "Everybody's been making an effort to be nice to her, but she just keeps moping around, and they want to have fun."

"I think I'll go talk to her," said Mary Anne. "I hate to see her sitting there all alone." She walked over to the apple tree and sat down next to Becca. "Hi," she said.

"Hi," said Becca, softly.

"Don't you want to play hopscotch?" asked Mary Anne. "Or softball?"

Becca shook her head and didn't say a word.

"Maybe you and Vanessa could pick some flowers and make a bouquet for Mrs. Pike," Mary Anne suggested. "Mothers like that kind of thing."

"*My* mother loves flowers," said Becca. "But she doesn't love me." She sniffed, and a tear worked its way down her cheek.

Mary Anne winced. How could she have said something so dumb? "Of course she loves you," said Mary Anne. She reached over and stroked Becca's arm.

"Uh-uh," murmured Becca. "She doesn't. If she did, she wouldn't have gone off and left me all alone. Daddy doesn't love me either, and neither do Jessi or Aunt Cecelia. Squirt loves me, but they made him go off and leave me, too. I'm all by myself."

"Oh, Becca," said Mary Anne. "You know that's not true. Everybody loves you, and they'll be back soon. In the meantime, you're not alone. Look at all the people in this yard!"

Becca looked up. "They're a family," she said. "I'm all by myself, but they're a family. They have a mommy and a daddy who love them, and they love each other."

Mary Anne couldn't stand it anymore. "Becca, come sit on my lap," she said. "I think you need a big hug."

Becca crawled into Mary Anne's lap, and Mary Anne gave her a bear hug. Becca started to cry. "I'm not going to stay here anymore where nobody wants me," she said, between sobs. "I'm going to run away."

"Run away?" asked Mary Anne, surprised. "Where to?"

"To my house," Becca said. "I'll wait there until my family gets back."

Mary Anne thought for a moment. Becca seemed very determined, as if she'd been thinking over this idea for a while. And even though Mary Anne knew the plan was ridiculous, she decided to play along for a while. As sitters, we've learned that sometimes this is the best way to let children find out for themselves that their ideas may not be practical. "Do you have a key to your house?" Mary Anne asked.

"A key?" asked Becca, looking surprised. "No, I don't. And I'm sure the house is all locked up. I didn't think of that." She was quiet for a moment, and then her face brightened. "It doesn't matter," she said. "I'll just camp out in the backyard. Charlotte and I have been talking about doing that for a long time. It'll be fun." She sounded like she was trying to convince herself. "Will you help me get some supplies and things?" she asked Mary Anne.

"Sure," said Mary Anne. "Let's see, what will you need?" She ticked off items on her fingers. "Sleeping bag, flashlight, pillow — "

"Cookies," added Becca. "Lots of cookies. And I'll bring my Little Mermaid bag, with all my stuff in it."

Mary Anne nodded. "Good idea," she said. "How about if you go inside and start getting everything together?"

Becca seemed to take it for granted that Mary Anne would help her. It didn't seem weird to her at all that her baby-sitter was helping her "run away." It would almost have been funny, Mary Anne told me later, if it weren't so sad. Mary Anne sent Becca inside to pack her Little Mermaid bag. Then she filled Mal in on what was happening. "I'm sure she'll get halfway down the street and turn around," said Mary Anne. "As soon as she realizes that sleeping outside by herself is going to be even lonelier than being here."

But Becca was already a step ahead of Mary Anne. A few minutes later, when she was sitting on the porch surrounded by her "camping supplies," Becca turned to Mary Anne and said, "I think I'll be lonely out there all by myself."

Mary Anne agreed, relieved to hear that Becca was already realizing how impractical her plan was. But Becca wasn't ready to give up yet.

"So will you come with me?" Becca continued.

What could Mary Anne do? She'd been playing along, and now she was going to have to go even further. "Um, okay," she said. She went back to Mal for a conference. The two of them talked the situation over, and decided to call Dawn to see if she'd come over and take Mary Anne's place at the Pikes'. That turned out to be fine with Dawn, so before long Mary Anne and Becca were on their way.

As they walked along with their supplies banging against their knees, Becca talked excitedly about returning to her own house. "I'll be able to sit on the back porch if I want to," she said. "And tomorrow morning I'll wake up in my own yard. And then when everybody comes home, I'll be there waiting for them. They'll be surprised, won't they?"

Mary Anne nodded. "They sure will," she answered.

When they arrived at the Ramseys', Mary Anne and Becca headed for the backyard and set up their camp. It was late in the afternoon by then, and beginning to grow dark. Becca lay down on her sleeping bag to try it out. "This is pretty comfortable," she said. "Right?"

Mary Anne was lying on another sleeping bag. "Well . . . " she replied, "I feel a rock underneath my back. But I'm sure I won't notice it when I fall asleep."

"Do you think it's going to get really, really dark out here?" asked Becca, in a subdued voice.

"It'll be dark, all right," said Mary Anne. "And we might hear some funny noises. But I don't think there are too many dangerous wild animals around here, so we'll probably be safe."

"Wild animals?" asked Becca. She was silent for a few minutes. "You know," she said finally, "I feel a rock under *my* back, too. I don't think I'm going to sleep well tonight."

"Oh, well," said Mary Anne. "That's what

97

camping out is like sometimes. Now, how about some yummy dried fruit? That's all we have for dinner. Too bad we couldn't bring along any of that lasagna Mrs. Pike told Mal to warm up for dinner."

"Lasagna?" Becca asked in a tiny voice. "I love lasagna."

Now Mary Anne was quiet for a little while. Then she spoke up. "You know," she said in a whisper, as if she were about to confess something to Becca, "I'm kind of scared about sleeping out here all by ourselves."

"You are?" asked Becca. "Me, too!" She paused, and then said, "Maybe you won't mind very much if we don't camp out after all. I think maybe I'd rather go back to the Pikes'."

Mary Anne smiled. "That sounds fine to me. I bet they'll be glad to see you."

She and Becca sat up on their sleeping bags and talked for a while about how it feels to be left out or left behind. Mary Anne told Becca about a time in third grade when her father had gone away on a business trip, and how lonely she'd felt then. By the time they returned to the Pikes', everybody was sitting around the dinner table, about to dig into a delicious-smelling pan of lasagna. They greeted Becca as if she'd been gone for years, and Becca looked happier than she had all weekend. Mary Anne had saved the day.

CHAPTER 11

I fastened my mom's jet necklace around my neck and turned to face Stacey. "How do I look?" I asked.

She gave me the thumbs-up sign. "Awesome. That black velvet dress is perfect for you. And I love the way you braided your hair. Quint's going to think you look gorgeous."

I hadn't told Stacey — or anyone else — about my plans for The Talk with Quint. Somehow I felt very private about it. And, in fact, I'd nearly forgotten about it with all the excitement. Now I vowed to have The Talk after Quint's performance, which was drawing closer. In a few minutes I'd be on my way to Juilliard, and within a couple of hours the program would be over. Then it would be T-time.

I tried to put it out of my mind. I wanted my attention to be focused on Quint and his dancing that night. This was a very special event for him, with a large, sophisticated New York audience. I wanted to watch every step he danced so I could talk to him afterward about the program. I knew he'd want to hear my opinion.

I took a deep breath and tried to shove away my nervous thoughts about that stupid Talk. I thought instead about how my sister was doing, back at the Pikes'. I'd called to find out, and Mal had filled me in on Mary Anne and Becca's "camp-out." I was confident that Becca was doing just fine.

I checked myself in the mirror once more, then asked Stacey to walk me downstairs to get a cab.

I arrived at Quint's apartment right on time. Quint had already left to get ready for the performance, and the plan was that I would go to Juilliard with his parents and Tyler and Morgan. They were dressed and ready to go when I arrived. "Don't you look nice," said Mrs. Walter. "Honey, come look at Jessi," she called. Mr. Walter walked into the living room with Morgan and Tyler behind him.

"You look lovely," he said.

"You look like a princess," said Morgan breathlessly.

I felt a little uncomfortable. Here were the Walters, acting warm and friendly toward this person they thought was their son's girlfriend.

And here I was, ready to — well, ready to break up with him, I guess. I blushed. "You look very nice, too," I said. "Morgan, I love your party shoes."

She spun around on her toes. "I'm a princess, too," she announced.

Tyler snorted. "Right," he said. "Princess Pest."

"Am not!" yelled Morgan.

"All right, all right," said Mr. Walter. "Let's not get into a squabble right now, kids. It's time to go see your brother dance."

"Yea!" shouted the kids, their fight forgotten.

We headed downstairs and piled into a cab. I held Morgan on my lap, and Mr. Walter held Tyler on his. We were squished in together, and everybody was joking about it. "Whose elbow is in my ear?" asked Mrs. Walter, chuckling.

"Don't tickle me!" squealed Morgan, when I put my arms around her waist.

"I don't think I have any feeling left in my legs," said Mr. Walter. "You're getting to be an awfully big boy, Tyler."

"My corsage is getting squished," said Mrs. Walter. She was wearing a delicate pink corsage that Mr. Walter had given her for the occasion.

I tried to join in the fun, but I felt awkward.

The Walters were treating me like one of the family, but I didn't really feel I deserved that kind of treatment. I just hoped they wouldn't hate me when they heard about my Talk with Quint.

Fortunately the cab ride wasn't too long, and soon we were pulling up near Lincoln Center. The Juilliard School is part of a complex of buildings at Lincoln Center. If you're standing on Broadway (or rather, on the sidewalk *next* to Broadway), you see this gigantic fountain in the center of a courtyard. Surrounding the courtyard are three concert halls, built out of white marble. There's the New York State Theatre, which is home to the New York City Ballet and the New York City Opera. These neat-looking honeycomb-shaped lights hang on its front. Then there's the Metropolitan Opera House. If you look through the big arched windows, you can see these gorgeous tapestries that hang in the lobby. The Met, as New Yorkers call it, is where the opera and the ballet perform. The third building is Avery Fisher Hall, which is where the New York Philharmonic Orchestra plays.

Juilliard is kind of across from all those buildings, and you can enter it by climbing a set of stairs near the fountain. The school is built out of that same white marble, so it looks as if it belongs with the big concert halls.

I stood looking at the scene for a moment. I get shivers whenever I see Lincoln Center, because dance and music seem so alive there. I mean, it's like the center of the universe for dancers and musicians. You know, I'm not always positive I want to be a ballerina when I grow up, but when I look at Lincoln Center I feel there's nothing else I'd rather be. Just to see all the people flocking into the theatres and concert halls, eager to listen and watch, makes being a ballerina seem very important. I mean, people need beauty in their lives, and ballet can certainly provide that.

Wow! I'm getting philosophical here, and a little off the track. I just wanted to give you an idea of how exciting attending an event at Lincoln Center can be.

Anyway, the Walters and I walked up the stairs and into Juilliard. "I think the theatre's this way," said Mr. Walter, leading us down a hall. Quint's performance was going to be held in the Juilliard Theater, which was built just for student performances. "Here we are," said Mr. Walter, stopping at a set of doors. Lots of other people were clustered around the entrance. Some were dressed up, like the Walters and me, but others were wearing T-shirts and jeans. I figured most of the T-shirt people were Juilliard students.

I peeked into the theatre. It was beautiful!

It's a small theatre — it holds maybe two or three hundred people — but it's really pretty. It has a red carpet and red upholstered seats, and wood paneling on the walls.

"The panels are for acoustics," said Mr. Walter, glancing over my shoulder to see what I was looking at. He pointed at these wooden panels that stuck out of the walls near the stage. "You know, so music sounds good in here."

I nodded. "It's a neat theatre," I said.

"Ready to go in?" he asked.

"I have to go to the bathroom," whispered Morgan loudly.

I had to go too, but I wasn't about to announce it. "I'll take her," I said. "I noticed the bathrooms down at the end of the hall."

"We'll go ahead and sit down then," said Mr. Walter. "Our seats are in row D in the upper level. I'm sure you'll be able to find us."

Morgan and I hurried to the bathroom and used it (I took the opportunity to check the mirror to make sure my braids weren't coming out), and then headed back to the theatre. As we approached the double doors, I looked ahead at the crowd of people and stopped short.

"What's the matter, Jessi?" asked Morgan.

"N-nothing," I answered. "Let's go on in." I hurried her into the theatre, my heart pounding. Guess what I'd seen? Or maybe I should say *who*? It was Red. Or at least someone who looked an awful lot like him. I couldn't believe my eyes. Could he and Frank really be following me? And would they actually follow me to a ballet performance?

I found my seat and settled down. Then, as I waited for the curtain to rise, I tried to relax. I told myself I was imagining things. I told myself jewel thieves don't *go* to the ballet. I told myself I was safe with the Walters. And you know what? It worked. Kind of. At least, when the curtain *did* rise, and Quint and his classmates came out, I was able to forget about Frank and Red and allow myself to be swept up in the beauty of the dancing. These students were *good*. And I mean really *really* good. They looked like professionals.

Mrs. Walter leaned over and whispered to me, "Doesn't Quint look terrific?" Her eyes looked kind of teary. "I'm so proud of him," she added.

I nodded. "Me too," I said. And it was true. I was incredibly proud of Quint. I was also jealous! He's getting such great training and it really shows. He'll have no trouble becoming a professional if that's what he wants.

The first half of the program seemed to go by in a flash, and before I knew it the curtain had lowered for the intermission. I knew I should stay in my seat. I knew that if Frank or Red were there I shouldn't show my face. And I knew I'd only get scared if I saw them. But somehow, I couldn't help myself. "Excuse me," I said, standing up. "I need some air." I went out to the lobby, knowing I could be making a big mistake.

Guess what? I was right. It *was* a big mistake. I saw the man again and I was sure he was Red. How was I sure? Because he was with Frank. They were standing at the edge of the crowd, and I couldn't help staring at them. Until I noticed that Frank was looking straight back at me! Oh, my lord. That did it.

I practically *ran* back to my seat. And the rest of Quint's performance was, unfortunately, wasted on me. I just couldn't concentrate on the dancing. I kept wondering where Frank and Red were sitting, and why they'd come to the theatre. I searched every face in the audience, but I didn't see them. That made me nervous, since I figured they must be sitting *behind* me. Yikes!

Finally, the program ended. I joined the rest of the audience in a standing ovation, but my heart wasn't in it. I kept peering behind me until I saw Mrs. Walter giving me a funny glance. As we filed out of the theatre, I kept a sharp lookout for Frank and Red, but they were nowhere to be seen.

The Walters and I went backstage to see Quint, and everybody made a huge fuss over him. I did my best to act normal and to appear excited about his performance, but all I was waiting for was a chance to get Quint to myself for a moment. When I did, I blurted out what I'd seen.

"*Now* do you think we should go to the police?" I said. "I mean Frank and Red are following us. This is getting scary!"

"Can you *prove* they're following us?" asked Quint.

"Well — no."

"Then it's not time to go to the police yet. Look, I'll tell you what. Come to my house first thing tomorrow, and *we'll* follow *them* for as long as it takes. Okay?"

"Okay," I said. "And — Quint? You were really awesome."

He looked down at his shoes. "Did you really think so?" he asked shyly.

"I really did," I said. And I meant it.

CHAPTER 12

I woke up the next morning to the sound of rustling paper. I yawned and rubbed my eyes and looked over at Stacey, who was sitting cross-legged on her bed. "Morning! What are you doing?" I asked.

"Reading the Sunday *New York Times*," she said."It's kind of a New York tradition to spend Sunday morning this way."

"Can I have the funnies?" I asked.

She giggled. "Sorry. No funnies. The *Times* is a *serious* paper. No funnies. Or horoscopes. Or Ann Landers."

"So what do you *read* in there?" I asked.

"Oh, there's lots to read. Right now I'm reading about a new photography exhibit at the Museum of Modern Art. Dad and I may go see it today, after we have brunch."

Stacey is *so* cosmopolitan.

"I have to go to Quint's," I said. "Today's our last chance to try to figure out what Frank and Red are up to." I'd told Stacey about seeing them at the performance the night before. She had been a little worried, but she seemed to think Quint and I could try some more detective work, as long as we were careful.

"Mind if I call Becca again?" I asked. "I'll leave your dad some money for the phone bill."

"Go ahead," said Stacey. "I know you're worried about her."

After I'd washed my face and brushed my teeth, I dialed the Pikes' number. Mallory answered. "Hi," she said. "How's your weekend in the big city going?"

I told her about Quint's show, and about seeing the jewel thieves there. She was fascinated. "I am *so* jealous," she said. "You're in the most exciting city in the world, you get to eat lunch at the Plaza and go to performances at Juilliard, *and* you have a mystery to solve." Mal loves mysteries, and I knew it was driving her crazy to be left out of this one.

"I'll tell you everything when I get home tonight," I said. "I sure hope I can say that Frank and Red are safe in jail by then." I paused for a second. "So how's Becca doing?" I asked.

"Much better," said Mal. "She and Mary Anne came back by around eight last night, and Becca had ice cream with everyone else. Right now she's eating pancakes."

"Her appetite is back, I guess," I said.

"Definitely. Want to talk to her?"

Mal put Becca on the phone. "Hi, Jessi," said Becca. "I'm having pancakes with ketchup on them. Byron told me it's good, and he was right!"

"You sound like you're beginning to have a good time," I said.

"Uh — " Becca's voice changed all of a sudden. "I miss you, Jessi. I feel so lonely here. Why did you all have to go away and leave me?" She gave a little sniff.

I rolled my eyes. "I'll bring you a present when I come back," I said, ignoring her dramatics.

"Really? Cool! 'Bye, I have to finish my pancakes." She hung up the phone.

I stared into the receiver. Then I smiled and shook my head. At least Becca was starting to enjoy herself. That was one less worry for me. Now I could concentrate on Frank and Red. And on the Talk I had to have with Quint, which I hadn't had the night before. I decided to make Frank and Red the first priority, since I wasn't particularly eager to start the Talk. It could wait awhile longer.

I arrived at Quint's by ten that morning. He was waiting for me. "Listen," he said. "I had a great idea. I was reading this detective book last night, and there was this scene where the detective searched through the suspect's garbage looking for clues."

"Ew!" I said.

"Yeah, it's kind of gross," admitted Quint. "But it worked! He found a letter that practically *proved* the guy had committed a murder."

"What are we going to look for?" I asked. "I mean, we won't find emeralds and rubies in the trash."

"Of course not. But we may find something incriminating. You never know."

"Well, okay," I said, shrugging. "Since we don't have a better plan."

"While we're searching we'll keep an eye out for the thieves," said Quint, "and if we see them leave the building we'll follow them." He led me outside to where the garbage is collected, next to his apartment building.

"Double ew!" I said, looking at the pile of plastic bags and the overflowing garbage cans.

Quint held his nose. "Let's get started," he said. He grabbed one of the bags and pulled it open. I peered over his shoulder. The bag was full of orange peels, coffee grounds, and something that looked like dog barf. "Ew," said Quint.

Just then I heard someone whistle, and I

turned around. It was Frank! He was standing on the curb, facing the street (luckily we were hidden behind the garbage), and Red was with him. He was whistling for a cab.

"Come on!" I said to Quint. I pulled his sleeve and he dropped the garbage bag. We hit the curb just as Frank and Red were getting into a cab. I saw another cab right behind theirs, and I threw up my arm. It pulled up and I shoved Quint into it. "Follow that car!" I said to the driver.

I have *always* wanted to say that. I couldn't believe I actually had the chance.

Quint looked at me admiringly. "That was cool, Jessi. You really acted fast."

"Thanks," I said. I was keeping an eye on Frank and Red's cab. Our driver was staying right behind it. He had a little smile on his face.

"Playing cops and robbers?" he asked, looking at me in the rearview mirror.

"Kind of," I said. "Whoa, watch out! They're speeding up." He hit the gas to follow them, just making it through a yellow light. Their cab was moving fast, but we stayed behind it. I could see Red's hair, bright as a carrot. We followed the thieves down Central Park West to Columbus Circle where the traffic zooms around this big plaza. Then they turned left onto Fifty-seventh Street. We turned, too. After a few blocks, their cab slowed down. It pulled to the curb on the corner of Fifth Avenue. "Pull over!" I said to the driver.

"Here," Quint said, handing him some money. "This should cover it."

"Thanks, buddy," said the driver. "Good luck with your game. Hope you catch those robbers!" He smiled at us indulgently. We clambered out of the cab, watching Frank and Red the whole time.

They were already halfway down the block. We followed behind "at a discreet distance," as the detective books say. They were strolling along slowly, looking into store windows. They stopped at one, and looked more closely. Lots of other people were window-shopping, so we were able to inch our way pretty close to Frank and Red without being noticed. I could even hear snatches of their conversation.

". . . diamonds are *huge!*" said Frank.

"That ring there must be worth . . ." said Red.

I exchanged excited glances with Quint. It was obvious that the thieves were "casing the joint." (That means they were checking out the merchandise and the layout of the store, so that they could make careful plans about their robbery. In "case" you were wondering.)

I looked into the store window. Wow! The display was lined with black velvet, and jewels of all kinds were sprinkled over it. Emerald earrings the size of marbles. Diamond-studded watches. Necklaces sparkling with rubies. Ropes of pearls. The stuff almost looked fake, but I knew better. There must have been thousands of dollars worth of jewelry in that one window.

I was so busy looking at the jewels that I missed the next part of Frank and Red's conversation, but then I saw them look at each other and shake their heads. They started walking again. "They must have decided the jewels at this store aren't worth it," I whispered to Quint.

"Either that or they've realized the security is too tight," he whispered back. "Come on, we're going to lose them." He grabbed my hand and pulled me along.

Frank and Red continued to stroll for a couple of minutes, and then they stopped short at another set of windows. I looked at the name of the store. "Heathe and Sons, Jewelers!" I said. "Wow. Do you think they're planning to rob Heathes'?"

Quint shrugged. "There's a lot of great jewelry inside, from what I've heard," he said. "Look — they're going in!"

"Come on," I said. I marched up to the door that Frank and Red had just entered, and opened it. Quint followed me inside. "Awesome," he said, looking around. There was kind of a hush in the store, even though it was crowded. And it had a certain smell, like all kinds of expensive perfume mixed together. People were standing at the counters, holding up diamond necklaces and trying on rings. Glass cases held beautiful crystal glassware.

"May I help you?" asked a man, stepping from behind a counter. He gave us a funny look, as if he wondered why two kids our age would even *be* in Heathe's.

"Uh-uh," said Quint. He sounded nervous. He couldn't think of anything to say, and neither could I. Were we supposed to tell him we were following a pair of jewel thieves who might be planning to rob his store?

A security guard approached us and stood next to the first man. "Okay, kids, where are your parents?" he asked.

"Uh," said Quint.

"We better go," I hissed in his ear. "We lost them, anyway." It was true. Frank and Red were nowhere to be seen by that time. We turned and left. (The security guard followed us to the door.)

In the cab on the way back to Quint's, we both fell silent. I was feeling humiliated, and I guess he was, too. Some detectives we were. What chance did we have of solving the case before I had to leave New York?

CHAPTER 13

Saturday

I think the Great Becca
Crisis may finally be
drawing to a close. Of
course, it got worse
before it got better,
but at least it now
looks like she may be
feeling a little less
abandoned. And I
don't mean to sound
conceited, but I think
I had a lot to do with
her working out some
of her feelings. I really
understood "where she
was coming from," to
quote a psychologist
I once heard on the
radio. And I think
Becca appreciated that.

117

Claudia was scheduled to sit at the Pikes' on Sunday. She'd only be sitting for Claire, Margo, Nicky, and Becca, though, since Mr. and Mrs. Pike were taking the older kids to that concert in Stamford.

"This job is going to be a breeze," she said to herself as she got ready to head for Mal's. "No triplets calling each other names. No Vanessa spouting poetry. Just me and the little ones." Then she thought for a moment. Four "little ones" could be quite a handful. Especially when their ages ranged from five to eight and a half. She was going to need an activity or a project to keep them busy, and it would have to be something they would all enjoy doing.

Claud looked around her room. Being an artist herself, she loves to come up with art projects for kids. But what? She looked at a box of pastels, and shook her head. "Too expensive," she said. "I'll be sorry if I bring those and they get used up." A few tubes of acrylic paint were next to the pastels, but Claud figured they'd be too messy and too hard to clean up. "Papier mâché?" she asked herself. "No, takes too long to dry and the kids get impatient." She glanced at a pile of magazines and thought about collages, but remembered how hard it can be to clean sticky glue off even *one* child.

Then Claud's glance happened to land on a poster she'd put up over her bed. It was a fantasy illustration with lots of color and action. A beautiful maiden was caught in the clutches of a dragon, and a handsome prince was about to rescue her. We'd noticed that picture during our last meeting, and had talked about why the *princess* is always the one to get rescued. I remember Kristy saying that "just once," she'd like to see a prince who needed help.

Anyway, when Claud noticed the poster, she was struck with a great idea. "Dragons!" she said out loud. "We'll make dragons." She checked her watch and saw that she had only fifteen minutes to organize everything. She bustled around her room, grabbing art supplies. She pulled a box of poster paints out from under the bed. She rummaged through her closet until she found a shoebox that held buttons, old wooden spools, and other stuff she'd collected. In a cubbyhole of her desk was some glitter, and a bag of yarn was stashed in her sock drawer.

Then she dashed downstairs to check the garage. There, in the cardboard recycling bin, she found a few empty paper towel tubes, several oatmeal containers, and some strong corrugated cardboard that could be cut and painted. "There, all set," she said. She packed everything into an old red wagon and headed over to the Pikes'.

"Claudia's here, Claudia's here!" yelled Margo when she saw Claudia trudging up the driveway. "What did you bring?" she asked Claud. "Presents?"

"Nope," said Claudia. "Art supplies."

"Cowabunga!" shouted Nicky from the porch. "Are we going to make a mural?"

Claudia shook her head.

"What are we making?" asked Byron. He had run into the yard, along with Adam and Jordan.

"You guys aren't making anything this time," Claud said to the triplets. "You have plans today, remember? This is for the little kids."

"Boo," said Adam.

"Yeah, boo," echoed Jordan.

"We'll do something next time," Claudia told them. "And you're going to have a great time at the concert."

"Hi, Claudia," said Mal, who had followed the triplets outside. "Looks like you're all prepared for today."

"I hope so. How's Becca doing?"

"Much better," said Mal. "She ate about

forty-five pancakes this morning."

"I ate a hundred-'leventy-seven!" said Claire proudly.

"I ate a gazillion," added Margo. "Well, not really. I only had three."

"Three pancakes should give you plenty of energy for our project," said Claudia.

"What is it?" asked Becca. She had arrived on the porch by that time. "What are we going to make?"

"I'll tell you soon," said Claudia. "After the others leave. That way it can be a surprise for them when they come back."

It took awhile for Mr. and Mrs. Pike to round up their concert-goers, but before long everyone was loaded into the car. Claud, Becca, Margo, Claire, and Nicky stood in the driveway and waved good-bye to them until they were partway down the street.

"Tell us now!" said Nicky. "They're gone, so now we can start."

Claudia smiled. Bringing along a project had been a great idea. None of the kids seemed to mind being left behind, since they had something special of their own to do. "Okay," she said. "Why don't you help me unload the wagon, and I'll tell you what we're going to make."

Claire reached into a paper bag and pulled out some glitter. "Fairy dust!" she cried.

Becca found the yarn. "And beautiful hair for a doll," she said.

"Paints!" exclaimed Margo, pulling out the poster paints. "All my favorite colors."

Nicky reached in and pulled out the paper-towel tubes. "Hoo-hoo tubes!" he shouted.

"Hoo-hoo tubes?" Claudia asked, puzzled.

"That's what we call these," Nicky said. He lifted one to his lips and made a sound through the tube. "Hoo-hoo!" The other kids cracked up, and so did Claudia. Then everybody grabbed a tube and started hoo-hooing. Claud noticed that Becca was hoo-hooing as loudly as anyone.

"Okay, you hoo-hoos," said Claud, after the noise had gone on for a few minutes. "Time to get started. Guess what we're going to make."

"Dolls?" asked Becca.

"I know!" said Claire. "A little town, with people in it."

"A nature scene!" cried Margo.

"No, dummy," said Nicky. "A robot!"

"You're all wrong," said Claudia. "And Nicky, don't call your sister a dummy."

"Sorry," said Nicky to Margo. "So what are we making?" he asked Claudia.

"Dragons," she replied.

"Yea!" shouted the kids.

Then Becca said in a small voice, "But I don't know what a dragon looks like."

Claud heard a certain tone in Becca's voice that made her think Becca might still be feeling a little lost. She hurried to explain. "It looks like anything you want it to look like," she said. "Dragons can look like dinosaurs or horses or salamanders. They can be purple or red or green or all colors mixed together. They can be big or they can be baby dragons. It's up to you."

"I'm going to make the biggest dragon in the world," said Nicky. "Big enough to eat Stoneybrook." He started to pull supplies out of the wagon.

"Hold on," said Claudia. "How about if we bring this stuff into the garage, where it won't matter if we make a mess?" She helped the kids set up in the garage, and then sat back to watch. She was amazed, she told me later, at how creative they were. Kids are like that. As long as nobody tells them that they can't do something, they'll try anything. They used all the supplies Claud had brought, and added a few things of their own. Nicky found his collection of Popsicle sticks and used them for spines, and Margo brought out some of her Legos.

Becca sat happily in the middle of all the

activity, making a baby dragon that she named Charlotte after the spider in *Charlotte's Web*. Claud saw no sign of the sad Becca who had moped and cried for so long. "It was almost like she'd forgotten she wasn't a Pike," Claud told me later. "She acted like part of the family, and the others treated her that way, too."

Building the dragons took quite a while. When they were done, the kids started to play "Dragon Kingdom," a game they made up on the spot. It involved picking a King and Queen of the dragons and then having dragon parties.

Claudia was so busy with the project that she forgot to keep track of the time, and before she knew it the Pike station wagon was pulling into the driveway. At that same moment, my parents arrived to pick up Becca.

"Mama!" Becca cried, running to give our mother a hug.

"Whoa," said my mom. Becca was covered from head to toe with green paint.

"Having fun?" asked my dad.

"Definitely," said Becca. She ran back to the garage to get her dragon. "See what I made?"

"Terrific," said my dad. "Now, how about if you get cleaned up so we can go on home."

Becca's face fell. "I don't *want* to go home,"

she said, pouting. "I'm having a good time here!"

Mal, who had climbed out of the station wagon, gave Claudia a Look and both of them had to stifle their laughter. I guess nobody can stay sad for long at the Pike home.

CHAPTER 14

Half an hour had gone by since we'd left Heathes', and Quint wasn't speechless anymore. Now he was mad.

"I just can't believe it," he said. "Don't we have any rights? They can't make us stay out of a store like that."

We were sitting on a ledge outside Quint's building. We'd just gotten out of the cab, but instead of going upstairs we'd sat outside to talk for awhile.

"I know," I said. "It's not fair."

"Do you think it was because we're African-American?" Quint asked. "I mean, maybe that's why they didn't trust us."

"Well, I might think that," I said, "except that the guard was black, too." I know prejudice exists, of course. But this time I didn't think it had anything to do with what had happened. "It's probably just because we're kids. They thought we'd start running around and bump into one of those cases filled with crystal glasses or something."

"Right," said Quint, with a grin. "That would have been quite a sight, to see thousands of dollars worth of glass breaking all over the place."

I laughed. "Or maybe they thought we'd put our faces against the jewel displays and fog up the glass."

"Pretty dumb," said Quint, shaking his head. "I mean, we're not five years old, you know?"

"They sure treated us like we were."

We sat silently for a moment.

"So what about Frank and Red?" asked Quint. "Do you think they were just casing the joint, or do you think they actually might have been about to rob the store?"

I gasped. "That's right," I said. "The robbery could be going on at this very moment. And it would be that guard's fault, for making us leave. We could have figured out a way to stop the thieves." I pictured Frank and Red stuffing handfuls of jewels into a bag while employees sat helplessly in the background, tied up with ropes. I imagined Quint and me sneaking up behind the thieves and pretending we were the cops.

Then I visualized the headlines in the next morning's paper. HEROIC TEENS FOIL DES-

PERADOES, one would say. JEWEL HEIST JINXED BY JUVENILES, another would shout. Maybe we'd get medals from the mayor, or maybe the store owners would let each of us pick out a reward from the jewelry cases. I pictured myself surprising my mother with a beautiful pair of diamond-and-sapphire earrings.

I was so busy with my daydreams that I nearly jumped out of my skin when a car horn blasted nearby. I looked over at Quint. Our conversation had died, and he was just sitting, staring moodily at the sidewalk. Suddenly I realized this was as good a time as any for our Talk. After all, I'd be leaving soon. I had to get it over with. As I thought about how to start, I remembered a Talk I'd had with this boy Daniel I'd met at Shadow Lake, when the BSC was on a vacation together. Daniel and I had become friendly, and I was beginning to worry that he wanted to be more than friends. I guess I was also feeling guilty about Quint, just like I had when I'd gone to that dance with Curtis Shaller.

Anyway, when I had this Talk with Daniel, I was completely embarrassed because it turned out he *was* only interested in me as a friend. He had a girlfriend in Boston, where he came from. Still, it had been a good talk, and we did end up agreeing to be friends. I hoped my Talk with Quint would go as well.

I took a deep breath. "Quint?" I said. "We need to talk. About us." I had this funny feeling in the pit of my stomach, and my hands suddenly got sweaty.

"About us?" repeated Quint. "What do you mean?"

Uh-oh. Now I had to follow through. "Well," I said. "I've really had a good time with you this weekend. I fact, I have a great time with you whenever we get together. But I'm not sure — I mean, I don't know if — "

"If you want to be committed to being my girlfriend?" Quint asked.

"Yes!" I said, relieved. "That's it, exactly. I mean, I think we're kind of young for a long-distance relationship."

"I've been thinking the same thing," replied Quint, "but I didn't know how to talk to you about it. I never know what to do when there's a dance at school, for instance. Is it okay for me to ask another girl, or should I just not go?"

I thought of Curtis. "I went to a dance with another boy," I confessed. "But I felt guilty about it."

"Oh, Jessi," said Quint. He gave me a sympathetic look.

Quint is the *nicest* boy. I hope he'll still be around when I decide I'm ready for a real relationship. "I hope we'll always be friends," I said.

"Me too," said Quint. He took my hand. "Jessi, could I kiss you just once more, for old time's sake?"

I blushed and nodded. Then Quint leaned over, but just as I was closing my eyes, I heard a car door slam. My eyes popped open, and over Quint's shoulder I saw Frank and Red walking away from a cab. I clutched Quint's shoulder. "It's them," I hissed, and he turned around.

The two men didn't *look* like they'd just pulled off a big jewel heist. They weren't carrying bulging bags over their shoulders, and they didn't seem to be nervously watching for the cops. They walked into the building next to Quint's, as calmly as you please.

Quint and I exchanged a look, then jumped up and ran into *his* building, not calmly at all. We burst into his apartment and headed straight for the TV room.

"Jessi! Jessi!" called Morgan, as we ran past her. "Come look at my Barbie!"

"Not now, Morgan," I said.

"Quint!" yelled Tyler. "Will you play Monopoly with us?"

"Maybe later!" Quint replied.

He herded me into the TV room and closed the door behind us. We ran to the window and looked across the way. We could see into the room where we'd first seen Frank and Red, but it was empty. "Darn!" said Quint. "Do you think they went out again already?"

"Let's wait a minute," I answered. "Maybe they're in another room."

We sat quietly for a few minutes, but Frank and Red didn't show up. Then Quint said, "I have an idea. What if we went to their door, pretending we have to make a delivery or something? We could get a look around the apartment, and maybe figure something out."

"I don't know. That sounds dangerous. After all, they know what we look like, don't they? They might let us in just to trap us."

"Hmm," Quint said. "Maybe you're right. We could wear disguises, though. Then they wouldn't know who we are. I could wear my dad's glasses, and you could borrow this Halloween wig of Morgan's."

"But what would we be looking for in there?" I asked. "I mean, there probably aren't going to be piles of jewels just lying out in plain sight."

"No, but maybe we'd see a map of one of the stores, or a plan or something. Or maybe we could trap them into saying something incriminating."

"You mean, talk about diamonds and see how they react?" I asked.

"I guess," Quint answered. "Oh, I don't know. All I know is that I want to solve this mystery and make sure they don't get away with anything."

"I just wish we could go to the police," I said. "If only we had more evidence."

"That's exactly what I'm saying," agreed Quint. "Maybe the only way to get more evidence is to get into their apartment."

By this time we were both seated on the floor, stretching. Ballet students and dancers do that any time they have a free moment. It's second nature. I had stretched my legs as far apart as they could go, and my head was nearly on the floor between them. Quint was doing this complicated pretzellike stretch that's supposed to be good for your back. We'd both forgotten — for a moment — to watch out the window.

Suddenly I heard Frank's voice, loud and clear. "You double-crossing weasel!" he said.

Quint and I sat up *fast* and looked out the window. There, across the way, were Frank and Red standing in the middle of that living room.

"I'm not double-crossing you, Frank," said Red. "It's just that I'm not so sure about this plan of yours."

"What are you talking about?" said Frank.

"We've worked on this plan for three months. It's foolproof."

Quint and I exchanged looks. He raised one eyebrow, and I raised both. Something weird was going on here. This fight sounded very familiar.

"So you say," Red said, shrugging. "But I just don't know."

Frank looked mad. "What are you afraid of, you chicken-livered lily-hearted wimp?"

Red burst out laughing. "No, no, no," he said. "It's *lily-livered* and *chicken-hearted*! Check your script."

Frank was laughing, too. He picked up a sheaf of papers and leafed through them. "I can't believe I did that," he said. "I thought I knew these lines backward and forward."

"*Backward* is right," said Red, still laughing. "Come on, let's try again."

As you can probably imagine, by this time Quint and I were in total shock. "Script?" I whispered to him.

"Lines?" he whispered to me.

Then we cracked up. We laughed until our stomachs hurt and tears rolled down our cheeks. We'd been fooled by a pair of actors.

CHAPTER 15

"Quint! Jessi!" called Mrs. Walter from the other room. "It's almost four o'clock. Don't you have a train to catch, Jessi?"

I caught my breath. I'd been laughing so hard that I couldn't speak. "Thanks, Mrs. Walter," I called back. I turned to Quint. "Well, our mystery has been solved, I guess," I said. "Can you believe it?"

"Maybe we'll see them on TV sometime," he said. "They sure are good actors. I believed every word they said."

"You chicken-hearted, lily-livered — " I said, imitating Frank's growly voice. We cracked up again. "Well, I guess I better get going," I said. "Want to walk me downstairs to catch a cab?"

"I'll be honored to, my dear," said Quint in a fake English accent. He gave me a bow. "But first," he said, in his normal voice, "there's something I meant to do before. Can I do it now?" He looked into my eyes.

I felt a little shiver. Quint is the first boy I ever kissed, so it seemed right for him to kiss me one last time now. "Sure," I said. I closed my eyes and leaned toward him.

The door burst open. "Jessi!" said Morgan, running into the room. "Do you *have* to leave?"

"We want you to stay," added Tyler, who had run in behind her.

I looked at Quint, smiled, and shrugged. He shrugged too, and smiled back at me. It was as if we were speaking without words. My shrug had meant, "Well, we missed out on that kiss again." And his had meant, "Oh well, I guess it wasn't meant to be." Or something like that. One thing I knew for sure, though. Our smiles had meant "We'll always be friends, no matter what."

Morgan and Tyler were both hugging me at once. I hugged them back. "I really have to go, guys. But I'll miss you a lot, and I'll be back to see you very soon."

"Promise?" said Morgan, looking at me seriously.

"Promise," I said. I glanced at Quint and gave him a nod, to tell him the promise was real. "Do you guys want to come down and help me get a cab?" I asked Morgan and Tyler.

"Yes!" they cried.

Quint and I walked into the living room. Mr. and Mrs. Walter were sitting on the couch, reading a newspaper. The Sunday *New York Times*, of course. "Thank you for everything," I said. "I had a wonderful weekend."

"Well, it was wonderful to see you, Jessi," replied Mr. Walter.

"We hope you'll come again soon," added Mrs. Walter.

"Thanks," I said. "I will."

Quint and Morgan and Tyler and I went downstairs together. We stood on the sidewalk, looking up the street to see if any cabs were coming. "I'll never forget this weekend, Jessi," said Quint.

"Me neither," I said. "It was great. And I'm so glad I got to see you perform." I smiled at him.

"Hey, look at that man's hair," said Morgan suddenly. She was pointing at someone behind us. "It's a funny color."

"Morgan," hissed Quint. "It's not polite to point. And it's not polite to talk about people's looks." He turned to see whom she was pointing at, and I turned, too.

It was Red! And he looked like he'd heard everything Morgan had said. Fortunately, he was smiling. "That's okay," he said. "I know my hair is a funny color. But I like it. It's

136

different." He gave Quint a closer look. "Say, don't I know you from somewhere?" he asked.

"Uh . . . um," said Quint.

"Taxi!" I shouted. I saw one coming down the street, and I threw up my arm. I hated to leave Quint in such a weird situation, but hey, I had a train to catch! " 'Bye!" I said to him. I gave him a quick kiss on the cheek. Then I waved to Morgan and Tyler and jumped into the cab. I grinned out the window at Quint as we pulled away. I knew he would be fine talking to our "jewel thieves."

I gave the driver Mr. McGill's address and sat back to enjoy one more ride through Central Park. I was really beginning to feel comfortable in New York City. I day-dreamed a little as we drove, about living in New York as a member of a world-famous ballet company. Would I rather live on the East Side or the West Side? I decided the West Side would be better, because I'd be nearer to Lincoln Center. But I'd have to be sure to find an apartment near Central Park, so I could walk through it every day.

Stacey was waiting for me when I arrived at her dad's apartment. "We don't have much time," she said. "Can you pack in fifteen minutes?"

"No problem," I said. I threw all my stuff into my bag, grabbed my toothbrush from the bathroom, and told her I was ready to go.

"We're not in *that* much of a hurry," she said, laughing. "How did things go this morning?"

"I'll tell you on the train," I replied. I didn't mean to sound mysterious, but I wanted to tell her the whole story without rushing through it. I was dying to see her reaction when she found out who Frank and Red really were.

Mr. McGill rode with us in the cab to the station. "Jessi, it was nice having you," he said. "Even though I didn't see you much. You were pretty busy this weekend."

"Thanks for having me," I said. "And thanks a lot for that special lunch." I'd have to remember to tell Stacey why I'd asked to eat at the Palm Court. I was still embarrassed about it, but it was part of the story.

When the cab pulled up at Grand Central Station, I spotted a sidewalk vendor halfway down the block. "Stacey," I said, "I just remembered that I promised to bring Becca a present. Can you wait a second while I look over there?"

Stacey and her dad walked with me to the cart and stood to one side talking as I made my choice. I found the perfect thing right away. "All set!" I said, once I'd paid the vendor. We entered the station and Mr. McGill walked us down to the track where our train was waiting. He gave Stacey a big hug and made her promise to take care of herself. "Come back soon, boontsie," he said. Stacey blushed, but she smiled, too.

The train left Grand Central right on time. Stacey and I had put our luggage on the overhead rack and were settled into our seats. "So?" she asked. "Tell all!"

"Let's see," I said. "Where should I begin?"

"Start at the beginning again," she said. "Even though I've heard some of it before. That way, you can practice telling the rest of the BSC."

So I did. I started with the part in which Quint and I were playing I Spy out the window. I told her about the fight we'd seen, and how Frank and Red had seen us and maybe even heard our names. Then I told her about the next two days, how we had followed them — and how they had followed us. "Guess why we wanted to go to the Palm Court?" I asked Stacey, in the middle of my story. She laughed when I confessed the reason.

Then I told her how we'd gotten kicked out of Heathes', and how we'd gone back to Quint's feeling like we'd *never* solve the case. And finally, I revealed the Dramatic Conclusion. ". . . so it was all from some kind of script!" I said. "They were *actors*!"

Stacey looked shocked for a second. Then she cracked up. "That is the wildest story!" she said. "I never would have guessed."

"I know I should feel embarrassed to have been fooled like that," I said. "But it's just too funny. If they only knew what they put us through!" I remembered "Red" talking to Morgan and Quint. He seemed like a really nice guy. He probably would have gotten a kick out of our story.

"So what did you get for Becca?" Stacey asked, when she finally stopped laughing.

I pulled out the gift.

"Oh, that is so, so cute," said Stacey. "She's going to love it."

"I think so, too," I said. I'd bought Becca a little troll doll. You know, the ones that are really cute in an ugly kind of way? It was dressed up to look like the Statue of Liberty, and it wore a red Miss-America type sash that said I ♥ NY in white letters.

Stacey and I talked all the way home. She told me her father had only gone to work for those few hours on Saturday, and had spent the rest of the time with her, doing special things. "That must be a record," she said. "I know how hard it is for him to stay away from the office."

Then I told Stacey about my Talk with

Quint. She was impressed with how well it had gone. "The important thing is that you'll always be friends," she said.

"I know. And I know I did the right thing, but I have to admit that I'm going to miss the romance a little bit."

"I bet you'll have another boyfriend before you know it," said Stacey. "What about Curtis Shaller?"

"He's okay. But I think I just want to be friends with him, too. At least for now."

Before I knew it, the train had pulled into the station. We were home. I glanced out the window and saw my entire family waiting for me on the platform. Stacey's mom was standing with them. I jumped off the train about two seconds after it stopped, and ran to hug everyone.

"Hey, welcome back!" I heard someone call from behind me. It was Kristy. She was running along the platform, with Mallory, Claudia, Mary Anne, and Dawn right behind her. "Sorry we're late," she said. "Charlie's car wouldn't start, so Watson ended up driving us."

I looked at the crowd that stood around Stacey and me. All our friends and family had turned out to meet us! It felt great to be home. I handed Becca her doll. "Here's your special New York present," I said.

"Thanks!" she cried, patting the troll's long hair. "I love it."

"How was your weekend at the Pikes'?" I asked.

"It was terrific! I had the best time. I can't wait to stay with them again."

I laughed. "That's great, Becca," I said, and grinned privately at Mal.

That night at home, I spent a long time on the phone. Here's who I called: Mallory, Kristy, Dawn, Mary Anne, and Claudia (to tell them about my jewel thieves), Stacey (to thank her for a great weekend), and Quint (ditto).

My converstation with Quint was really nice. We laughed a lot and confessed that we missed each other already. He pretended to be mad at me for leaving him alone with "Red," but he was only kidding. It turned out that "Red's" real name was David, and he was a really nice guy. He has a niece who's in Quint's ballet class, which is why he was at Juilliard the night before.

Just before we hung up, Quint invited me to his next dance performance, which would take place in the fall. "I'm glad we're friends, Jessi," he said in a soft voice. "I know we always will be."

"Me, too, Quint," I said. "Me, too."

About the Author

ANN M. MARTIN did *a lot* of baby-sitting when she was growing up in Princeton, New Jersey. She is a former editor of books for children, and was graduated from Smith College.

Ms. Martin lives in New York City with her cats, Mouse and Rosie. She likes ice cream and *I Love Lucy*; and she hates to cook.

Ann Martin's Apple Paperbacks include *Yours Turly, Shirley*; *Ten Kids, No Pets*; *With You and Without You*; *Bummer Summer*; and all the other books in the Baby-sitters Club series.

Look for Mystery #9

KRISTY AND THE HAUNTED MANSION

"This room is boring," said Jackie. He led the way back into the hall and into a third bedroom. This one had definitely belonged to a man. The furnishings were dark and heavy, and the bed, covered with a brown spread, stood solidly along one wall. This room had a big fireplace, and over it hung another portrait. This one was of a man, dressed in a tailcoat, looking very stiff. Jackie went closer and peered at the brass nameplate under the painting.

Just then, Bart and Charlie joined us. "Who's that guy?" Bart asked.

Jackie gulped. "It says his name is Owen Sawyer," he said in a whisper. He sounded frightened for some reason.

"That makes sense," said Charlie. "I think the name of the road we were on is Sawyer Road."

144

"Really?" asked Jackie. "Then this must be the Sawyer house!"

"So?" asked Buddy. "What does that mean?"

"It means — " said Jackie, "it means that this house is haunted!"

I heard several kids gasp. "What are you talking about, Jackie?" I asked.

"Shea told me all about it," said Jackie. "I thought it was one of his ghost stories, but maybe it's for real! People have seen all kinds of weird stuff happening here. Lights going on and off, doors that were locked hanging open, smoke coming from the chimney . . ."

Karen leaned forward. She loves ghost stories. "What else?" she asked.

"Sometimes people see a woman walking around, and they say it's the ghost of a woman who died in the area," Jackie finished. His face was white.

My heart was beating fast, but I knew I should jump in before Jackie got everyone *really* scared. "I'm sure those stories are nothing more than tales people made up for fun," I said firmly. "After all, there are no such thing as ghosts." At least, I thought to myself, I sure hope there aren't.

Read all the books
in the Baby-sitters Club series
by Ann M. Martin

#52 *Mary Anne + 2 Many Babies*
Who ever thought taking care of a bunch of babies could be so much trouble?

#53 *Kristy For President*
Can Kristy run the BSC and the whole eighth grade?

#54 *Mallory and the Dream Horse*
Mallory is taking professional riding lessons. It's a dream come true!

#55 *Jessi's Gold Medal*
Jessi's going for the gold in a synchronized swimming competition!

#56 *Keep Out, Claudia!*
Who wouldn't want Claudia for a baby-sitter?

#57 *Dawn Saves the Planet*
Dawn's trying to do a good thing — but she's driving everyone crazy!

#58 *Stacey's Choice*
Stacey's parents are both depending on her. But how can she choose between them . . . again?

#59 *Mallory Hates Boys (and Gym)*
Boys and gym. What a disgusting combination!

#60 *Mary Anne's Makeover*
Everyone loves the new Mary Anne — *except* the BSC!

#61 *Jessi and the Awful Secret*
    Only Jessi knows what's really wrong with one of
    the girls in her dance class.
#62 *Kristy and the Worst Kid Ever*
    Need a baby-sitter for Lou? Don't call the Baby-
    sitters Club!
#63 *Claudia's Freind Friend*
    Claudia and Shea can't spell — but they can be
    friends!
#64 *Dawn's Family Feud*
    Family squabbles are one thing. But the Schafers
    and the Spiers are practically waging war!

Super Specials:

5 *California Girls!*
    A winning lottery ticket sends the Baby-sitters to
    California!
6 *New York, New York!*
    Bloomingdale's, the Hard Rock Cafe — the BSC is
    going to see it all!
7 *Snowbound*
    Stoneybrook gets hit by a major blizzard. Will the
    Baby-sitters be o.k.?
8 *Baby-sitters at Shadow Lake*
    Camp fires, cute guys, *and* a mystery — the Baby-
    sitters are in for a week of summer fun!
9 *Starring the Baby-sitters Club!*
    The Baby-sitters get involved onstage and off in
    the SMS school production of *Peter Pan*!

Mysteries:

1 *Stacey and the Missing Ring*
    Stacey's being accused of taking a valuable ring.
    Can the Baby-sitters help clear her name?

147

 # 2 *Beware, Dawn!*
Someone is playing pranks on Dawn when she's baby-sitting — and they're *not* funny.

 # 3 *Mallory and the Ghost Cat*
Mallory finds a spooky white cat. Could it be a ghost?

 # 4 *Kristy and the Missing Child*
Kristy organizes a search party to help the police find a missing child.

 # 5 *Mary Anne and the Secret in the Attic*
Mary Anne discovers a secret about her past and now she's afraid of the future!

 # 6 *The Mystery at Claudia's House*
Claudia's room has been ransacked! Can the Baby-sitters track down whodunnit?

 # 7 *Dawn and the Disappearing Dogs*
Someone's been stealing dogs all over Stoneybrook!

 # 8 *Jessi and the Jewel Thieves*
Jessi and her friend Quint are busy tailing two jewel thieves all over the big apple!

 # 9 *Kristy and the Haunted Mansion*
Kristy and the Krashers are spending the night in a spooky old house!

Special Edition (Readers' Request):

Logan's Story
Being a boy baby-sitter isn't easy!

by Ann M. Martin

❏ MG43388-1	#1	Kristy's Great Idea	$3.25
❏ MG43513-2	#2	Claudia and the Phantom Phone Calls	$3.25
❏ MG43511-6	#3	The Truth About Stacey	$3.25
❏ MG43512-4	#4	Mary Anne Saves the Day	$3.25
❏ MG43720-8	#5	Dawn and the Impossible Three	$3.25
❏ MG43899-9	#6	Kristy's Big Day	$3.25
❏ MG43719-4	#7	Claudia and Mean Janine	$3.25
❏ MG43509-4	#8	Boy-Crazy Stacey	$3.25
❏ MG43508-6	#9	The Ghost at Dawn's House	$3.25
❏ MG43387-3	#10	Logan Likes Mary Anne!	$3.25
❏ MG43660-0	#11	Kristy and the Snobs	$3.25
❏ MG43721-6	#12	Claudia and the New Girl	$3.25
❏ MG43386-5	#13	Good-bye Stacey, Good-bye	$3.25
❏ MG43385-7	#14	Hello, Mallory	$3.25
❏ MG43717-8	#15	Little Miss Stoneybrook...and Dawn	$3.25
❏ MG44234-1	#16	Jessi's Secret Language	$3.25
❏ MG43659-7	#17	Mary Anne's Bad-Luck Mystery	$2.95
❏ MG43718-6	#18	Stacey's Mistake	$3.25
❏ MG43510-8	#19	Claudia and the Bad Joke	$3.25
❏ MG43722-4	#20	Kristy and the Walking Disaster	$3.25
❏ MG43507-8	#21	Mallory and the Trouble with Twins	$2.95
❏ MG43658-9	#22	Jessi Ramsey, Pet-sitter	$3.25
❏ MG43900-6	#23	Dawn on the Coast	$3.25
❏ MG43506-X	#24	Kristy and the Mother's Day Surprise	$3.25
❏ MG43347-4	#25	Mary Anne and the Search for Tigger	$3.25
❏ MG42503-X	#26	Claudia and the Sad Good-bye	$3.25
❏ MG42502-1	#27	Jessi and the Superbrat	$2.95
❏ MG42501-3	#28	Welcome Back, Stacey!	$2.95
❏ MG42500-5	#29	Mallory and the Mystery Diary	$3.25
❏ MG42498-X	#30	Mary Anne and the Great Romance	$3.25
❏ MG42497-1	#31	Dawn's Wicked Stepsister	$3.25
❏ MG42496-3	#32	Kristy and the Secret of Susan	$2.95
❏ MG42495-5	#33	Claudia and the Great Search	$2.95
❏ MG42494-7	#34	Mary Anne and Too Many Boys	$2.95

More titles... ▶

The Baby-sitters Club titles continued...

❑ MG42508-0	#35 Stacey and the Mystery of Stoneybrook	$2.95
❑ MG43565-5	#36 Jessi's Baby-sitter	$2.95
❑ MG43566-3	#37 Dawn and the Older Boy	$3.25
❑ MG43567-1	#38 Kristy's Mystery Admirer	$3.25
❑ MG43568-X	#39 Poor Mallory!	$3.25
❑ MG44082-9	#40 Claudia and the Middle School Mystery	$3.25
❑ MG43570-1	#41 Mary Anne Versus Logan	$2.95
❑ MG44083-7	#42 Jessi and the Dance School Phantom	$3.25
❑ MG43572-8	#43 Stacey's Emergency	$3.25
❑ MG43573-6	#44 Dawn and the Big Sleepover	$2.95
❑ MG43574-4	#45 Kristy and the Baby Parade	$3.25
❑ MG43569-8	#46 Mary Anne Misses Logan	$3.25
❑ MG44971-0	#47 Mallory on Strike	$3.25
❑ MG43571-X	#48 Jessi's Wish	$3.25
❑ MG44970-2	#49 Claudia and the Genius of Elm Street	$3.25
❑ MG44969-9	#50 Dawn's Big Date	$3.25
❑ MG44968-0	#51 Stacey's Ex-Best Friend	$3.25
❑ MG44966-4	#52 Mary Anne + 2 Many Babies	$3.25
❑ MG44967-2	#53 Kristy for President	$3.25
❑ MG44965-6	#54 Mallory and the Dream Horse	$3.25
❑ MG44964-8	#55 Jessi's Gold Medal	$3.25
❑ MG45575-3	Logan's Story Special Edition Readers' Request	$3.25
❑ MG44240-6	Baby-sitters on Board! Super Special #1	$3.50
❑ MG44239-2	Baby-sitters' Summer Vacation Super Special #2	$3.50
❑ MG43973-1	Baby-sitters' Winter Vacation Super Special #3	$3.50
❑ MG42493-9	Baby-sitters' Island Adventure Super Special #4	$3.50
❑ MG43575-2	California Girls! Super Special #5	$3.50
❑ MG43576-0	New York, New York! Super Special #6	$3.50
❑ MG44963-X	Snowbound Super Special #7	$3.50

Available wherever you buy books...or use this order form.

Scholastic Inc., P.O. Box 7502, 2931 E. McCarty Street, Jefferson City, MO 65102

Please send me the books I have checked above. I am enclosing $_____
(please add $2.00 to cover shipping and handling). Send check or money order - no
cash or C.O.D.s please.

Name _____

Address _____

City_____ State/Zip _____

Please allow four to six weeks for delivery. Offer good in the U.S. only. Sorry, mail orders are not
available to residents of Canada. Prices subject to change.

Join the new online Baby-sitters Club* on the PRODIGY® service.

*A Custom Choice℠ for the PRODIGY service.

TALK TO ANN M. MARTIN IN A WEEKLY COLUMN

READ ALL NEW STORIES STARRING THE BSC GANG

VOTE ON STORY ENDINGS

MAKE FRIENDS ALL ACROSS THE COUNTRY

TAKE POLLS AND PLAY TRIVIA GAMES

PRODIGY.
Interactive Personal Service

For more information, have your parents call

1-800-776-0838 ext.261

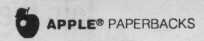